The Path to
REDEMPTION

A Journey to the End of the Earth

D1727226

Published by St Julian Books

ISBN
978-1-84396-676-0

Also available as a Kindle ebook
ISBN
978-1-84396-677-7

A catalogue record for this book is
available from the British Library and the
American Library of Congress.

Typesetting and pre-press production
eBook Versions
27 Old Gloucester Street
London WC1N 3AX
www.ebookversions.com

Bay of Biscay

FRANCE

Bilbao

Saint-Jean-Pied-de-Port

Roncesvalles

Larrasoana

Pamplona

Puente de la Reina

Los Arcos

...agún

Calzadilla de la Cueza

Carrión de los Condes

Frómista

Castrojeriz

Hornillos del Camino

San Juan de Ortega

Santo Domingo de la Calzada

Belorado

Nájera

Burgos

Logroño

Duero

Zaragoza

Camino de Santiago

Camino Francés
Camino Fisterra

Author's Note

Ever since I walked the Camino to Santiago de Compostela for the first time, nine years ago, I have been back, again and again. There is something addictive about the whole experience: the wonderful countryside; the majestic cities with their great cathedrals and palaces; the quaint little villages; the people of all ages, nationalities and backgrounds that one meets and the great sense of camaraderie that exists; the demanding physical effort; and, most of all, the spirituality. I decided to use the Camino as the backdrop for my story.

The two protagonists of the story, James and Maria, unbeknown to each other, are overcome separately by their feelings of guilt over the same event. They both try to find their way to forgiveness and redemption. Each of them discovers separately the Camino and its traditional role as a means of penance and atonement and they both resolve to walk it. They experience this, but they also find something very different.

I enjoyed writing this short novel during the difficult and unforgettable times that the Covid pandemic has created for us all. I would like to thank the members of my Creative Writing group: Maurice O'Scanaill, Edwina Portanier Brejza, Elaine McDougall, Brenda Murphy, Roberta Conrad and Chris Staff, all of whom offered helpful suggestions and, last but certainly not least, my wife, Sonja. She painstakingly read through the entire work, as did Rosa Guillaumier, and picked up many of the little errors that had inevitably found their way into the draft, often written late in the evening. Finally, I would like to thank my children, Andrew, Michael, Mark and Martine for their encouragement and Martin Bugelli, my editor, for the very meticulous and inspired review he carried out on my work.

The Path to
REDEMPTION

A Journey to the End of the Earth

Stephen Mangion

ST JULIAN BOOKS

To Marguerite

Chapter 1

He knew he was driving too fast, but it was one way of releasing some of the tension he was feeling. It had been a terrible day at the office. Everything that could have gone wrong, had. Even his last meeting with one of his best clients, with whom he had always enjoyed a good relationship, had gone badly. Instead of finishing work at around five as usual, he had needed to stay on for an extra hour or so, to try to resolve this last unexpected conflict. He was dying to get home, have a shower, get into his house clothes and fix himself a stiff gin and tonic. Then he hoped to be able to get back to his book and try to get the whole bad day out of his mind.

Night had fallen already but, he thought to himself, it was only a week to the start of spring, to which he was looking forward. The longer days that came with it meant that he could start to go for walks in the Maltese countryside, which he loved. His passion for walking had started some years ago when he was on holiday in Switzerland. He would go off for hours at a time, walking through the valleys of the Engadine, and sometimes up into the hills. He loved experiencing nature in all its forms – the trees and flowers, the forests, the wildlife, the vagaries of the weather and the smells and sounds of nature.

In Malta, he had slowly discovered some beautiful walks, either with breath-taking views like the Santi valley or Mtaħleb, or experiencing the raw power of the sea in a storm while walking along the coastline. He loved the little villages too, with their quaint old centres always dominated by the village church. He would walk through these villages and stop occasionally at one of the typical bars serving tea and coffee in glass tumblers, accompanied by delicious *pastizzi*, a traditional Maltese snack, made with pastry and filled with either ricotta or peas. He loved to sit in these bars and exchange views with the usually very colourful patrons of the bar, on country life, politics or whatever other topic caught his fancy at the time.

He brought his mind back to the present. He was still some distance from home, but he knew the road well, since he drove this way back on some days. Normally, he would take the circuitous, but more scenic, route home, but today he was in a hurry to get back. He had just passed the old cemetery when he rounded the bend down to his neighbouring village. As he came out of the bend, someone stepped off the pavement and into the road, right in his path. He reacted almost instantaneously, and his foot hit the brake pedal. However, he immediately realised that there was no way he was going to avoid hitting her, for in that split second, he saw that it was an elderly lady. As though in slow motion, he felt his car skidding to a halt, but nowhere near fast enough. The old woman appeared to be oblivious to her danger and just kept walking across the road. Suddenly, there was a dull, sickening thud as the car hit her, knocking her to the side of the road. She rolled for some few metres, came to rest on the sidewalk, and remained there motionless.

Time stood still. There was a sense of unreality coupled

with one of horror. He couldn't believe this had happened. He knew that he had been driving too fast but the way she had stepped out into the road without warning had made it difficult, if not impossible, to avoid her. At the same time, he was aware that his excessive speed would surely have made her injuries more serious. A flurry of thoughts shot through his brain. He would be blamed for this accident, even though he could not really have avoided it. He would be interrogated by the police, dragged through the courts and possibly even end up in prison. It would destroy his comfortable life. It was a nightmare scenario. He felt that he wanted to scream. A blackness descended over his eyes.

His brain attempted to rationalise what had happened. If only the woman had looked before crossing! How could he be blamed for something that he could not possibly have avoided? Maybe the woman was not too badly hurt after all … The sound the impact had made was quite muted. She was bound to be found in a few minutes in what was normally a fairly busy street, then she would be taken to hospital and hopefully recover. Then, blind panic took over again. After his initial sudden braking and the impact, his car had continued to roll forward slowly due to the slight slope in the road, but he was already beyond the point of the accident. He could no longer see the old lady's body, and all he could see ahead of himself was the dark, empty street, the trees waving gently in the breeze and the lights inside the houses. His right foot came to rest lightly on the accelerator pedal and slowly the car gathered speed and before he knew it, he was moving away down the road. He rounded another corner as he thought that surely no one saw what had happened. The woman would be found any moment now and all would be all right. He almost felt a strange sense of relief.

Later that night he awoke in a cold sweat. He had over-indulged in drink as soon as he got home. After his usual gin and tonic, he had downed a second one. He only fiddled with his food but drank two or three glasses of wine. The drink had an anaesthetising effect on him and this, plus the reaction to his experience, made him feel suddenly very tired. Therefore, he went to bed earlier than usual and tried to sleep. But sleep would not come. He took a sleeping pill and after a short while, he fell asleep, but woke up at around three in the morning. He realised immediately that he was not going to be able to fall asleep again. He felt wide-awake, even though he so badly wanted to sleep again and consign all the terrible thoughts to his subconscious, to oblivion.

The hours passed, he tossed and turned, trying hard to find solace and peace, but could not. At six, he gave up the struggle and forced himself to get up and to start getting ready for the day. As he did so, he started to feel hope spring up again. Surely, everything would be all right! It might turn out to be a non-event after all, so maybe, if it were to be reported in the paper at all, it would be a footnote on one of the middle pages. He snatched a hurried breakfast – much less than his usual fare – and then went to the garage. He looked at the front and sides of the car and he was relieved to see that there were virtually no traces of the accident, apart from a slight dent on the front left-hand side, near the headlamp. This gave him renewed hope that the lady might not have been hurt too badly. It was time for him to leave for his office. On the way, he stopped at the corner store as usual to buy the newspaper. Today, he was particularly anxious to see it.

Once back in his car, he started to look through it feverishly. Nothing on the front page, and nothing on pages two and three either. Then, there it was, on page four! The headline read *Hit and Run Accident in Naxxar*. He started to read the article and was immediately shocked by the opening sentence, which stated that the woman, Antonia Pace, had died of her injuries and that the police were actively seeking the author of this terrible accident.

The flimsy fabric of hope, which he had built up after the accident, collapsed in an instant. Suddenly, the enormity of what he had done, hit him. He had run over a pedestrian, an elderly lady, and because of his excessive speed, had caused her injuries that proved to be fatal. Instead of trying to help her, as he should have done, he had driven away. Who knows how long it had taken for someone to find her after the accident? Could her life have been saved had she been taken to hospital immediately? He could not believe he had done this. Whatever could have come over him? He had always regarded himself as an upright and conscientious man, and he would never have imagined doing something like this and yet, when it came to the moment of trial, he had failed badly. He threw the newspaper down in desperation. He could not finish reading the article.

He spent most of that day in a trance. However hard he tried to focus on his work, he could not. His thoughts kept coming back to the accident and that terrible moment when he realised that he could not avoid hitting the woman, and then the impact that followed. In his mind's eye, he saw the woman's face as she looked towards the car in a final moment of awareness, just before it hit her, and threw her body to the side of the road. He alternated between the deepest sense of guilt at what he had done and seeking some justification for himself in the woman's sudden appearance in front of him. His secretary, Lisa, must have noticed that something was wrong because she asked him whether he was feeling all right. He told her that he had not slept well the night before and was feeling rather under the weather. He wanted to bury this whole thing if he only could. Finally, at six, he was able to wind things up for the day and he started to head home.

He took the circuitous route home, as he could not face driving past the site of the accident. Driving by the sea calmed him down somewhat so, when he got home, he was able to follow his usual routine. After he had changed, he fixed himself a drink and went to sit out on the terrace, even though it was quite chilly outside. As he finished his first drink, he started to feel a bit better, and he took a second one for good measure. He tried reading but could not concentrate on his book; he tried watching television but soon gave that up. Finally, he thought he would find some peace in sleep, so he went to bed. While trying to sleep, he prayed for the first time in months, but it was of little avail. He drifted in and out of sleep and had obsessive dreams, which tormented him, making him relive those few terrible seconds, mixed in with other more mundane ones, to create a strange phantasmagoria.

The morning after, he was feeling tired and listless, and he had to make a big effort to get out of bed at the usual time. On his way to the office, he started to think about the lady he had killed. 'Was she married? Did she have any children?' he wondered. He had never finished reading the article in the newspaper through to the end, as he was so shocked and had just wanted to get rid of the paper as if it were red hot. He guessed that he could find out by getting a back number of the paper, or by searching on the internet, but his morbid curiosity finally gave in to his imperative need to try to block the whole thing out of his mind, especially the thought of learning about people to whom he had caused extreme pain. Once again, he went through the motions at work, and his colleagues did not detect anything very different or noteworthy in his manner. However, his secretary, who knew him better than most, was not fooled. She sensed that something was seriously troubling him from the little changes in his manner that only she could detect. However, she did not question him about it.

Driving back home that evening, the route by the sea relaxed him again, and he started to think about things a bit more rationally. He thought first about his situation: he could not possibly go to the police now. He would be hauled off to prison while awaiting trial for a fatal hit-and-run accident. Public opinion would be against him, especially since the victim was a helpless, elderly lady. No one would believe him if he said that she had almost thrown herself in front of his car. They would be sure to think that it was just an excuse to try to save his skin and cast the blame for the accident on his victim. He had no choice but to learn to live with the secret and hope that he would never be discovered – but how could he live with something like that on his conscience? Somehow, he had to find a way of finding repentance, not merely as a self-serving way to ease his misery, but in true repentance followed by atonement. Would he still be forgiven if he did this without admitting his guilt to the police and to society?

In the meantime, he had to find a way of preserving his sanity and his health. He would force himself to follow a strict regime, turning to the things that made him feel good. He would walk every morning before going to work and he would go to a gym in the evenings. He hoped that the hard, physical exercise would keep him healthy, both physically and mentally. Although he was a practising Catholic, he had not been to Confession for a long time, but he remembered the sense of relief he used to feel in the past, when he would tell the priest about the sins he had committed, sins, which in comparison with his current one, paled into insignificance. It would not be easy to tell a fellow human being what he had done, even if only to a priest who was bound by a vow of secrecy. Yet he felt that he must do that, and he resolved to contact his old friend and confessor, Father Joe, at his local church. He called him that very evening when he got home.

Father Joe must have been busy as he took a long time to answer but finally, he did.

"Hello Father. It's James… James Borg. How are you keeping?"

"Hello, James," Father Joe replied. "I'm well, but I have been really overburdened in these last weeks. Two of our young priests have been posted to another parish and I have had to take over most of their workload, but I am coping, with God's help. It's been a long time since we spoke, how are you?"

"Not too bad, Father, but I need to come and see you. When would be convenient?"

"How about tomorrow evening? Would you like to come round after work? Say around six."

"Thanks, Father. That would be great. See you tomorrow,

then."

He already felt a bit relieved after that phone call, as though he had taken a first positive step – but towards what?

Chapter 2

Maria Mallen was applying the final touches to her makeup. As she looked into the mirror, she felt pleased with what she saw. She was almost forty years old and she carried her years very well. Her skin was still quite smooth, with hardly any wrinkles and quite unblemished. She was tall and slim, thanks to the exercise regimen that she had always maintained, and she had a good figure. There was an almost girlish look about her, which made her seem a good bit younger than her years. A further thought crossed her mind: she felt a rush of satisfaction that she had recovered from the trauma of the separation, and eventual divorce, from her ex-husband, Tom Mallen.

A good three years had passed since then and she had slowly but surely learnt to cope with being single. It had not been an easy time. She had had a couple of relationships since her divorce, but nothing lasting. However, she was seeing someone again now. After the big disappointment of her first and only marriage, she was very wary about forming any serious liaisons. She was a passionate and exuberant person and she had many friends whom she used to meet often in the past. However, since her father's death twelve months ago and the diagnosis of her mother with incipient Alzheimer's Disease, all this had changed. She and Johanna, her only sibling who was three years older than she was, used to have to take it in turns to look after their mother on alternate days, since she was still living at home. During the day, the sisters had employed a nurse to stay with their mother until the early evening, but then they would take over from her and spend the evening and the night at their mother's home until the nurse's return the following morning. It was not easy but they had decided to try and keep their mother at home for as long as possible. However, they knew that when the illness eventually reached an advanced stage, they would inevitably, albeit reluctantly, have to place her in a home. As it was, their mother still had most of her faculties, but she was very forgetful, and would often be very distracted. Both of them did their best to engage her in conversation, as she could sometimes fall into long periods of silence and introspection, so they tried to involve her in activities that exercised the brain. They thought that this might help to slow the inexorable decline.

That day, it was Maria's turn to look after their mother. She had returned earlier than usual from the office in order to get herself ready. Her boss was very understanding, and he let her leave a bit earlier on the days when she was on duty. She worked as a secretary to the owner and managing director of a construction company. At the office, she was well liked and respected, and had become an indispensable member of the company. She had packed her overnight bag and was about to leave, when her latest boyfriend, John, called her. She was running late so she said she would call back once she got to her mother's home. She drove there and let herself into the house. The day nurse was expecting her somewhat impatiently, as it was a bit later than their usual hand-over time. After the usual pleasantries, the nurse left, and she joined her mother in the living room, where she was watching television. Maria hugged and kissed her mother, who kissed her back, and then settled down again on the sofa and went on watching her programme. Maria fixed her mother's usual cup of tea, took it to her and sat down near her. Just then, her phone rang. It was John. He had not waited for her to call him back. She told him to hold for a minute, going to the terrace at the back of the house to talk to him in private.

"Hello John. I wish you had waited for me to call you. I have just arrived at mummy's and I was just starting to sort things out for her. I would have called you in about thirty minutes or so," she said with some impatience.

"Really, Maria? You know, it's become quite difficult these last couple of months. You never seem to have any time for me! You're either at work or looking after your mother. When can we have some time together … and I don't mean, on the phone?" he said petulantly.

Maria groaned inwardly. He was starting to complain again as he had been doing practically every time they spoke in the last few weeks. It was getting on her nerves.

"You know how difficult it has been for me since mummy was diagnosed with Alzheimer's. Besides, I have been through a tough time since my divorce from Tom. When I went into that marriage, I thought it would be right, but it wasn't at all. In fact, it was disastrous and very traumatic for me, so please try and understand why I am so cautious about any new relationships."

"Are you comparing me to Tom?" he asked, angrily.

"No, I'm not, but I do not feel ready yet to take our relationship forward as fast as you seem to want me to do," she said, with some feeling.

He could not, or would not, understand her point of view. The argument went back and forth, getting more and more animated. Time passed and eventually, she had had enough. She had been very uncertain about her relationship with John for some time, and this was the last straw. She told him that this was the end. At first, he protested but then adopted a more conciliatory tone. However, she stuck to her decision and reiterated it was all over, and that she now needed to get back to her mother.

As she made her way back to the living room, she felt a cold draught, which was her first intimation of something being amiss. When she got there, her mother was no longer sitting on the sofa, although the television was still on. Maria called her name but there was no reply, and she assumed that her mother had felt tired and went up to her bedroom to rest. However, as she walked into the hall, she noticed that the front door of the house was open, which explained the draught. She moved quickly to the door and looked outside. It was quite dark but there was no one to be seen. Maria shut it and then thought to herself that perhaps the nurse must have forgotten to close it when she left. She went back inside and climbed up the stairs to her mother's bedroom. It was empty. She tried the bathroom. That too was empty, as were the other two bedrooms.

It was then that the penny dropped. Her mother had opened the front door, and probably walked out of the house! Suddenly, she was very worried. Her mother could be quite distracted and could easily wander off and get lost. She ran downstairs, went to the front door, opened it and looked up and down the street.

It seemed empty. The lights were on in most of the houses, no one could be seen outside. She walked fifty metres up the road in one direction – nothing there. Then she walked in the other direction. The trees that lined the street blocked most of the light of the moon and that of some of the streetlights as well, but she thought she saw something further down the road. As she hurried there and got closer, she realised that it was the body of a person lying face down, partly on the sidewalk and partly on the road. She moved as if in a dream with mounting horror and dread, she knelt near the body, and gently turned it over so she could see the face, although she already knew that it was her mother.

What had happened? Had her mother fallen on the sidewalk while walking out on her own in the dark? Then she saw a bloodstain spreading on her mother's jacket and realised that this was not the result of a mere fall; she must have been hit by a car. She finally came out of her state of shock, and shouted for help, fumbling for her mobile phone. She dialled the emergency number and screamed down the phone for an ambulance urgently, telling the person on the other side of the line that there had been a very serious accident. In the meantime, someone must have heard her screams. The door of one of the houses opened and a man came out to ask what the matter was. She screamed again, telling him what had happened, and he ran over to her while several other neighbours looked out of their doors or windows. Together, they tried to move her mother's body onto the sidewalk, while Maria felt for her mother's pulse. It was very weak indeed and her breathing was laboured and shallow. Frantically, she called her mother's name over and over again, but there was no response at all, except for a slight flicker when Maria took her mother's hand in hers. Other neighbours had meanwhile come out of their homes and started to gather around. They were speaking in low voices or whispers. After what seemed like hours, they heard the sound of an approaching distant siren. Finally, an ambulance drew up with lights flashing. Two paramedics sprang out of the ambulance with a stretcher, which they placed on the sidewalk beside her prostrate mother, and then very carefully lifted her on to it and into the back of the ambulance. Maria went up to them and insisted on riding in the ambulance with them to the hospital. They saw the state she was in and, after they asked her what her connection with the victim was, they helped her up into the ambulance, and helped her to the bench seat on one side of the ambulance.

They sped off with the siren blaring. Maria sat in a daze and watched with a feeling of unreality as the paramedics started to try to resuscitate her mother. She had to hold on to the bar next to the door to stop herself from falling off her seat as the ambulance took corners at high speed. Even in those tense and stressful moments, she somehow took in many of the details of the interior. She had never been in an ambulance before. It looked more highly equipped than she had imagined. The paramedics were going all out in their efforts to treat her mother. She felt utterly helpless and all she could do was pray that her mother would be all right, and that they would get to the hospital as quickly as possible. She willed the ambulance to move faster. After what seemed like an age, they slowed down as the ambulance drew into the hospital's A&E arrivals area. The door sprang open and the paramedics carried the stretcher out onto a gurney, which was wheeled at speed into the hospital building. Maria ran in after them, until one of the paramedics stopped her, saying that she would have to stay in the waiting area while they treated her mother. She wanted to ask him all sorts of questions but in her agitated state, no words came to her. He promised to keep her informed on how her mother was getting on, telling her to calm down and that all would be well.

At first, she sat down, but she was so tense that she soon got up and started pacing up and down. The waiting area was full of people and, although her mind was wholly occupied by her mother's condition, she couldn't help but notice the people around her. There was an elderly couple sitting very close together, holding hands and crying silently. A young man, with one arm in a sling, was trying to operate his mobile phone with just one hand, while a group of three young women chatted excitedly together. Another woman was alone and looking from left to right and, clearly, highly agitated as she herself was.

She was only now starting to comprehend what had happened. Her mother had wandered out of the house while she had been on the phone with John. She must have crossed the road and got run over. She could well imagine her mother just stepping out onto the road without looking, but how could anyone hit her and drive away? That was both incomprehensible and unforgiveable. Could it be that whoever it was had hit her mother, and not even noticed? No – that was impossible. The people in the car must have realised that they had hit someone, but still drove on. She thought of many names she could put to people who could do that, and what she would do to them! Then another terrible thought struck her. Had she been doing what she was supposed to be doing, this may never have happened. She should have been watching her mother at all times.

Although her mother still seemed normal in certain ways, she was quite clearly not so in many others. She should never have left her alone. Maria was slowly starting to realise that she too had some responsibility for what had happened. Then she put her hand to her forehead, as she remembered that, in her confused and upset state of mind, she had not yet told her sister about what had happened. She called Johanna, who said that she would be coming to the hospital immediately and would meet her at A&E. It only took her ten minutes to turn up and as soon as she saw Maria, she walked up to her and hugged her tightly. They sat down, and Johanna started to ask her all sorts of questions about what had happened. To Maria's surprise and relief, there was no recrimination from Johanna but that did not lessen the sense of guilt that Maria was feeling.

They sat there waiting together for an indeterminate period, losing all sense of time. Every time someone came out of the A&E, they would look up in expectation and hope. People came and went, and the night deepened. After several hours, the doors swung open once more and this time, a party of three persons in white coats came out and headed straight towards them. Both sisters stood up and waited in suspense. One of the three, clearly the doctor in charge, then told them that every effort had been made to resuscitate their mother, but her injuries were too serious, and she had succumbed just a few minutes before. Both sisters were distraught. Maria started to cry uncontrollably, bitterly blaming herself for what had happened. Johanna tried to comfort her, but to no avail. After Maria eventually recovered somewhat, Johanna drove her home and stayed with her till she was tucked safely into bed, kissed her goodnight and told her she would call her in the morning.

As Maria lay in bed, the full horror of what had happened struck her; the knowledge that her mother was dead, that the author of her death was unknown and at large and that, had she acted differently, her mother might still be alive. Dreadful thoughts flooded her mind and she found it impossible to sleep. She tossed and turned but could find no respite. At sunrise, she got out of bed and started to prepare herself for the day. She called her boss and told him what had happened. He was understandably shocked, even more so since he had met her mother a few times. He repeated many times how sorry he was and told her that she should take as many days off as she needed. Then, her phone rang, and it was the police. They told her that they needed to ask her a few questions, so she agreed to go to the Police Headquarters later that morning.

She arrived with some time to spare and was shown into a waiting area. After a few minutes, a police inspector came to meet her, gave her his condolences somewhat perfunctorily, and then asked her to accompany him. He took her to the chief inspector's office, who rose from his desk as soon as she entered the room. He went up to her, took her hand in his, introduced himself as Chief Inspector Robert Grungo and, much more warmly than the inspector, told her how sorry he was for her loss. He invited her to sit down and to tell him all that had happened. Maria started to recount it all – not that there was very much to tell. With some reluctance, she told him about her long conversation with her boyfriend and her mother leaving the house during that phone call without her noticing. Somehow, she found herself comfortable with talking to him about all this. There was something soothing about his manner, which made her feel that he would understand.

After some initial niceties, he asked her whether she had heard anything: the screeching of brakes, the sound of a car skidding, the sound of an impact, a scream, anything at all. She had to admit, once again, that she had been immersed in her phone call and had not heard anything out of the ordinary. He then asked her whether she had seen anything when she went outside. She confirmed that she had not. Someone must have told him that her mother suffered from Alzheimer's Disease, since he probed her about her mother's condition.

Maria tried to describe, as best as she could, how her mother had been behaving – her frequent lapses of memory and her occasional periods of confusion. She explained to him that she believed that her mother had probably just walked out of the house in search of something, and that she may have crossed the road without looking. However, she still railed against the unknown driver saying, in no uncertain terms, what she thought of someone who could hit, and then abandon, a person left injured on the road. He told her that they were doing their utmost to track down the culprit. They had analysed the brake marks left on the road, as well as some tiny fragments of paint left on her mother's body after the impact and had sent them to the forensic department for analysis.

Unfortunately, there were very few active CCTV cameras in the area and none of them had picked up the car that hit her mother. However, they had not given up and were looking further afield, to nearby streets where other cameras may have picked something up. He also told her that they had interviewed some of the immediate neighbours to ask whether anyone had seen or heard anything but, so far, they had drawn a blank. Finally, he asked her whether there was anything she needed, and she thanked him for this but said that there was not. She then said to him with great feeling, "Chief Inspector, please find out who did this. Find out who killed my mother."

"MsMallen, we shall do our very best. Rest assured of that. If you remember any other detail, please let us know. We shall keep you informed of any progress in our investigations," he said with a kindly and reassuring manner. Then he rose from his desk and accompanied her out of his office.

She returned home and phoned Johanna to tell her about her meeting with the Chief Inspector and to tell her that they needed to start organising the funeral for their mother. She knew that there would be a post-mortem carried out on her mother to determine the cause of death, and that the forensic experts would go over her body with a fine toothcomb, trying to glean anything that might shed some light on the culprit's vehicle. The Chief Inspector had informed her that the tests would be concluded the following day and then, she would be at liberty to start making funeral arrangements. Maria insisted on handling the arrangements herself as she felt a great responsibility. She started by calling a funeral director and explained what she wanted. He helped her organise all the details, such as placing an obituary in The Times, ordering the printing of the memorial cards to be handed out at the funeral, and a thousand and one other logistical arrangements. This occupied her for the next two days, so she had little time left to think.

On the day of the funeral, she rose early and waited for the car organised by the funeral director to pick her up and take her to the church. She arrived well before anyone else and looked over the church to see that everything was as it should be. There were beautiful flowers placed on and around the altar.

The choir, that the funeral director had engaged, was ready in the gallery. She sat down in the front row and waited. After a short while, her sister Johanna arrived with her husband and two children, and they all sat together. Little by little, the church started to fill up. Maria occasionally looked back along the nave 'of the church, and she could see friends and family congregating. As people sat down, a murmur of conversation could be heard, making Maria wonder how much of it was related to her failure to look after her mother. The word surely had got around about the circumstances of the tragedy. Soon, the Mass started, and Maria was quickly engrossed in it although occasionally her mind would wander back to the accident and her feelings of guilt. She had myriad images of the Mass, especially the priest's homily in honour of her mother, whom he described as a loving and constant wife and mother, who had dedicated her life to her two daughters. The choir sang some of her favourite hymns, creating a feeling of transcendence, with the presence of her extended family and friends who were there to honour her mother, and to support her.

After the Mass ended, she walked out of the church with her sister, following the coffin, which was being borne by the two grandsons and some family friends. Much as she wanted to get home, she had to go through the motions of meeting the mourners who had come to the funeral. She felt person after person kiss her on the cheek, and mouthing words of comfort that just washed over her. She felt she was starting to lose control of her emotions and she was dying to get away from the crowd that was suffocating her. However, there was still the ordeal of the burial to go through, but at least there were far fewer people to have to cope with, mainly family members and a few close friends. As she watched her mother's coffin being lowered into the grave, the finality of her mother's death really hit her. Various images flowed through her mind: her very earliest recollections of her mother reading her bedtime stories and kissing her goodnight; her first day at school when her mother had accompanied her there. She remembered vividly how she hadn't wanted to be left behind, but her mother had comforted and soothed her before leaving; her school-leaving ceremony, when her mother had clapped louder than anyone else as she went up to receive her certificate and how tightly she had hugged her afterwards; and her marriage to Tom and the wedding party, when her mother seemed to have a premonition of how it would all end. She remembered her mother's widowhood after her father died, and her constant care for herself and her sister and her two beloved grandsons. It was, apart from her father's, the first death at close quarters that she had encountered, and she was finding it hard to cope with, not least because of her part in it.

Her sister Johanna, and some close friends and family, came home with her after the funeral. After some time, they all left except for Johanna. Maria and her sister talked about old times, when they both lived at home, and about their more recent experiences with their mother's incipient dementia. Maria again felt somewhat relieved and grateful that her sister did not hold her to blame for what had happened. However, that did not change the fact that she felt that way herself.

That night did not go at all well for her, and neither did the next few nights. She found it hard to sleep and, more often than not, after she had slept, she would wake up at three or four in the morning, quite unable to go back to sleep. She tried various remedies – sleeping pills, herbal medicine, exercise – nothing worked. She started to resign herself to the fact that she could not sleep well and that she would have to learn to cope with this until perhaps the passage of time would make it more bearable.

Chapter 3

James woke up with a sense of purpose. He had fixed an appointment with Father Joe and he hoped that this would bring him some solace. He set off after work and got to St Anne's Church a few minutes before six. While he waited for his friend, he went over what he was about to disclose. A few minutes later, Father Joe appeared in his usual, slightly disheveled state, but James was so glad to see him. They went to his study together, to be able to talk in complete privacy. James had known Father Joe for many years, and he really had no idea how he was going to broach the subject that he had come to talk about.

Eventually he decided that he had to take the plunge. He asked Father Joe to hear his confession and then he told him all that had happened. He did not spare himself in the telling of it. He could have said that he could not have avoided hitting the lady when she stepped into his path, but he did not. He harped on about his abandoning the scene of the accident and the fact that, had he acted differently, he might have saved the victim's life. Father Joe tried to console him, but he did ultimately advise him to tell the police about his involvement in the accident. Much as James understood this, it was something that he simply could not face. He was still concerned that admitting his involvement in the accident would destroy his life forever, and he so badly wanted to find another solution. However, he felt some relief at having confessed his sin.

His life continued in much the same way. Generally, sleepless nights and difficult days, full of guilt and recrimination. He was starting to feel despair at the thought of the endless nights, when he got little or no respite from his daytime torments. His whole life had changed. He had lost the *joie de vivre* he had always had – the great feeling of excitement and energy he felt every morning as he awoke, just before going on his morning walk and with the whole day ahead of him.

The whole tenor of his life had changed. It had all become very negative, although there were a few moments when he would revert to his erstwhile persona – full of hope and excitement at what the day would bring – but these moments were few and far between. His work at the office was beginning to suffer as well. His level of focus and concentration had dropped significantly, and he was often distracted. Frequently, he thought about the old lady he had knocked down and killed, with a feeling of unreality and horror. He sometimes wondered whether she had a family – a husband, children, grandchildren – but the last thing he needed was to add a face and a life to the dead woman. He would not be able to cope with that, because it would make it so much more heart wrenching.

He had really been pushing himself at the gym since the physical exertion gave him some respite. In the lonely evenings, he tried to immerse himself in reading, so he went to his favourite bookshop and bought a whole lot of new books, which he picked largely after a cursory look at their title and résumé. At first, he avoided his friends, but he felt the need to confide in someone other than his confessor. His best friend Paul was the obvious choice. He called Paul and asked him over for a drink.

Paul arrived bang on time as always. James was glad to see him, since they had not met for some time. They went and sat on the terrace, taking advantage of the unusually mild weather for that time of the year. After the usual pleasantries and catching up on the last weeks, James started to broach the subject that was troubling him. He could not possibly tell Paul the whole story, even though he trusted him implicitly, but he was afraid that it would diminish him in his friend's eyes, so he approached the matter at a tangent.

"Paul, I've been going through a hard time. I'm not sure what the matter is but I just can't sleep at night and rarely manage to relax."

"I'm sorry to hear that, James. Can you put your finger on what you think is the cause?" said Paul, with obvious concern for his friend.

"I can't really put it down to any one thing. It's a series of issues that have been worrying me for some time. But I don't know what to do," explained James.

Paul was quiet for a few seconds, then he said, "We all go through periods like that sometimes, but we can help ourselves to get out of it."

"But how? I've tried all the usual things – exercise, my hobbies, medication. Nothing worked," said James, somewhat plaintively.

"Maybe you're lonely. It's about time you got yourself another girlfriend. Ever since you split up with Eva, you have been on your own. I would find it pretty challenging to live on my own without a partner. With all its faults – and I don't always find it easy living with Mary – marriage has its plusses. How long ago has it been since you split up?"

"It's been almost nine months since Eva left and I have never seen her again since then. I still miss her, but I think that it was never going to work out with her. We were just too different – too opposed. I must admit I do feel that life is passing me by. I would have loved to have a family by now, you know, a wife and children, like you. I am already forty-six. Most men would have brought up their children already by now."

"Have you considered getting help, like professional help, I mean?" Paul asked, hesitantly.

"Not yet. But I might."

Paul sensed that James was finding it hard to get to grips with whatever it was that was really troubling him or, at least, to talk about it. While he wanted to help his friend, he did not want to intrude or put pressure on him. He steered the conversation away from James's troubles and instead, they talked about things of mutual interest, such as reading, music, countryside walks and their past relationships before Paul's marriage. Slowly a warm glow settled over James, partly due to the pleasant memories evoked as they reminisced about their past, and partly thanks to the wonderful malt, which they were drinking. James had been saving a 35-year-old Cardhu single malt for a special occasion and, if ever there was one, this was it. They promised each other they would meet again soon, and Paul said that next time round he would ask James over to his home, as his wife Mary would love to see him too.

James tidied up and had a light dinner. As it was still relatively early, he settled himself in front of the television, as he felt like having a very simple evening, which needed no effort from his side. The news was on, and he watched all the usual fare, dominated as always by local politics, then the international news and followed by a cultural programme that did not particularly interest him. He started to surf the different channels and he stopped on the National Geographic Channel where a programme was about to start. At first, still thinking about his friend's visit, he was only half focused on it, but soon, he started to pay more attention. It was a travel documentary about a pilgrimage in Spain. There were some amazing images of wide, open countryside, mountains, plains and small villages. The narrator was describing a walk, which started in the south of France, and which extended all the way to a city in the west of Spain. He found the images captivating and he started to focus more and more on what was being said.

The narrator explained the legend that the remains of St James the Apostle had been discovered in the west of Spain sometime in the ninth century, and this had given rise to a pilgrimage, with pilgrims coming from Spain itself and from further afield to visit his tomb. He had never felt close in any way to his namesake saint, yet somehow this struck a chord with him now. He learnt how St James had reputedly gone to Spain to preach Christianity to the people of Galicia, which was then an important Celtic Druidic centre. However, after a couple of years, he had returned to Palestine after having largely failed to convert the people. The legend became even more unbelievable after that. Following his death, some of his followers were said to have taken his remains back to Galicia to bury him there. Much later, in the ninth century, a shepherd had reputedly seen a star, or stars, shining on a field, which led him to believe that this was an indication of the location of the apostle's remains.

All this sounded very fantastic, and yet, this had started a process involving thousands, if not millions, of pilgrims who over the centuries had come from all over Europe to try to get close to one of Christ's closest companions. The narrator went on to say that the pilgrims were not just poor, ignorant people, but that many members of the nobility and the great European families had made the trek to the city of Santiago in Spain.

Some did it out of devotion or simple piety, but many did it out of a sense of atonement for their sins. Many were ordered by their confessors to undertake this pilgrimage as expiation for their sins. The programme then focused on some present-day pilgrims, who included the whole range – from young people with rucksacks and bandanas to middle-aged and older people. They described their experiences while walking the 'Way', which they called "the Camino". James got quite involved despite himself and his worries. When the programme finally finished, he went to bed, deep in thought.

That night he did not sleep for long either, not only because of his usual demons, but also because of the thoughts provoked by the programme he had watched. Many of the images he had seen brought to life feelings that had been dormant since the accident. Once again, he felt the excitement of discovering new places on foot, of a walk that went in one direction only, towards a goal, never once turning back on itself and with a destination at the end of it. He had heard the comments of the persons interviewed who spoke of the great sense of camaraderie that they had encountered on the walk. He saw the little villages and the great cities through which the walk passed, threading its way from the south of France, over the Pyrenees and across all the northern part of Spain. He thought about the reasons driving people to do this. He could hardly begin to imagine what such an undertaking this would have been in the Middle Ages, and even in more recent times, before the days of air travel. Pilgrims would have had to start from their home, wherever this was, walk to their destination and then walk all the way back again. He understood that an experience like this would have given them the time to think deeply about their lives, and the physical suffering and deprivation that it entailed would surely have been a form of atonement for their sins, perhaps bringing forgiveness with it. He promised himself determinedly that he would find out more about it.

The day after, when he had finished from work, he browsed the internet for more information. He learnt that the Way, or the Camino, followed many different routes, almost all of which led to the city of Santiago de Compostela. He read that the origin of the name may have been connected to the shepherd's vision of a group of stars shining over the field where the apostle's remains were interred. He remembered enough of his schoolboy Latin to know that *campus* meant 'field' and *stellae* meant 'stars'. The shepherd's vision had come at an opportune moment, since it was during the *Reconquista,* when the Spaniards had begun to push back the Moors who had occupied most of their country for centuries. They were gradually winning back all their territory. They imagined that St James was spearheading their struggle to take back their land from its occupiers. The importance of the pilgrimage grew, especially after Muslim hordes took over and occupied Jerusalem, denying Europeans that other important pilgrimage route. The Camino reached its heyday in the 16th and 17th centuries but then started to diminish in importance. Yet, strangely enough, in the latter half of the twentieth century, there had been a resurgence, and the number of pilgrims was now back to its erstwhile level. Of course, many of the people who nowadays walked the Camino did not do so for religious reasons or as penance. Some did it because it was simply a long and wonderful walk, while others did it because it was a way of meeting people, and potentially, a partner. There were those who did it for health reasons, or who simply wanted to enjoy and appreciate the Romanesque and Gothic architecture and art in the towns and villages on the way.

Since pilgrims came from all sorts of directions towards Santiago, there were many, different ways. Some of the routes start in the south of Spain, in Seville or Granada, and others in the North, from Irun or San Sebastian. There is another from Lisbon, but it appeared that the road most travelled was the so-called 'Camino Frances' that sets off from a small village on the French side of the Pyrenees called St Jean Pied-de-Port. From there, the Camino crosses the Pyrenees and then passes through the famous cities of Pamplona, Burgos and Leon before reaching Santiago, some eight hundred kilometres away. Once again, James went to bed with a mixture of thoughts. His living nightmare, which would not go away and was not getting much better was on one side, while, on a more positive note, the pilgrimage he had just been reading about was on the other.

When he awoke the following morning, he decided to get hold of a guidebook or two about it. In his searches on the internet the night before, he had come across the titles of a number of guidebooks. He was not sure which one he should buy but, after some further research, he found out that there was an organisation based in London called the Confraternity of St James. Its mission was to help pilgrims intending to walk the 'Way'. He sent them an email asking for help in choosing a guidebook, and then after a rushed breakfast, left for the office.

He went for his mid-morning coffee in the cafeteria in his office building, feeling like he needed a bit of a break. The place was full, but he shared a table with two ladies whom he did not know. They were chatting together animatedly, and he realised they were complaining about what they regarded as the breakdown in law and order in the country over the past few months. One of them referred to the record number of traffic fatalities there had been so far, such as the recent hit-and-run accident. He felt a cold shiver go up his spine when he heard one of them say,

"It must be terrible for her two daughters. I heard one of them discovered her mother's body lying half on the sidewalk and half on the tarmac. What a horrible shock that must have been!"

"I do hope the police catch the bastard who did it," her companion replied, grimly.

"I heard on the news that they had very few leads to go on, unless this is just the usual excuse to cover their incompetence!"

"I cannot understand how anyone could have the heart to have done this. The least they could have done is stop and get help. I surely would have …"

"I guess the driver must have panicked and just driven away. I know that we both feel we could not do something like that, but then again, we have never been in that situation ourselves, God forbid that we ever are! One can never truly understand a person's feelings and actions unless one has been through the same experience."

James couldn't bear to listen any further to this discussion, even though the last statement had made him feel ever so slightly better. He downed the rest of his coffee in one gulp and went back to his office and worked until quite late. That evening he resumed his research into the Camino and, the more he learned about it, the more real it appeared. From a purely academic exercise, it had gradually begun to change to something that he might consider attempting. Apart from the attraction it held for him as a keen and accomplished walker, it would allow him to get away from his current surroundings and, most importantly of all, to perhaps begin a process of atonement and to help him find the peace that was now missing in his life.

Chapter 4

Maria arose early, as usual, and started to prepare herself for the day. She was returning to work after having spent a few days at home after the funeral. Nothing much had changed. If anything, it was getting worse. Her nights were full of troubled dreams that inevitably woke her up, after which she would spend hours listening to the chimes of the bells of the nearby church, which rang maddeningly every fifteen minutes. It had never kept her awake in the past, as she had become accustomed to it over the years, but now it did. She would try hard to push all thoughts out of her mind, but she never could. After endless tossing and turning, through sheer exhaustion, she would finally fall into a fitful sleep. Mornings would find her unrested, with each day becoming successively harder.

To make matters worse, John kept calling. The first time it was to commiserate on the death of her mother but, while she thanked him coolly for his condolences, she made it clear that she did not wish to talk to him ever again and stopped answering his calls. Johanna had told her that he had been at the funeral, but she herself hadn't seen him and was glad of this. She didn't blame him for what had happened, but he would be associated in her mind with her mother's death forever, since he had been the cause of her momentary, fatal distraction.

Today, however, her feelings were more mixed. On the one hand, she was glad to be going back to her job and meeting her colleagues, while on the other, it was her first real contact with people she knew, other than her sister Johanna, after the funeral. When she got to the office, her boss, Arnold Cassar, came to greet her. He hugged her and she appreciated this gesture. Although they had always had a good working relationship, he was a very reserved person who rarely showed his feelings openly, but on this occasion, he did. She was both surprised and pleased about that.

Once again, he told her how sorry he was and reminisced about the few times he had met her mother. Her emotions were reawakened by his compassion, and with the tears welling up in her eyes, she had to make a big effort not to cry. Arnold took her by the arm and walked her to her room. As they walked through the office, her workmates all expressed their feelings in different ways. Once she was alone, one of her best friends, Greta, walked in. She had seen Maria at the funeral but once again, she hugged Maria, took her hand and told her how very sorry she was. They talked for a while then Greta suggested that they meet for a drink after work.

Maria tried to lose herself in her work and, after some initial difficulty, she found that she had managed to become quite involved, despite herself and her troubles. Before she knew it, the working day was over, and she made her way to Greta's room. They left the building together and went to their favourite bar in the nearby square. It was not very full since there was still an hour or so to go before peak time. They found themselves a quiet table at one end and sat down. Greta started the conversation going, concernedly asking Maria,

"What a terrible shock this must have been for you. How are you feeling?"

"Not great! I cannot get over it and I feel responsible for what happened," Maria replied in a low voice

"Why should you, dear? You and Johanna have been so good to your mum over these last years, especially since your dad passed away."

"I do feel responsible, Greta. There is something you don't know and which I'll tell you, but please keep it to yourself because I feel so bad about it. On the day mummy got run over, I was supposed to be looking after her. While I was there, John called me on my mobile. I moved to the terrace to talk to him in private, as I knew that mummy did not approve of him. You know how protective she had become towards me after my marriage broke up. Anyway, John and I got into an argument, and I got carried away. We were at it for some time and when I ended the conversation and went back to the living room, mummy was not there.

I looked all over the house for her, and then saw that the front door was ajar. I wasn't sure at first whether I had left it open myself when I arrived, or whether the nurse had when she left. I did look outside but saw nothing. After I searched all over the house again, I realised that she must have walked out of the house after all. Johanna and I have been worried about this because, although mummy was reasonably OK at most times, she could be very distracted and unfocused at others. I walked up and down the street and saw her body lying at the side of the road. It was horrible."

"Oh my God! That's so awful. My poor dear," Greta said,

putting her hand over Maria's and pressing it tightly.

"Had I been with her, as I should have been, none of this would have happened", wailed Maria.

"Oh no! Don't say that. It would only have taken her a moment to leave the house. You could have gone to get her a cup of tea or needed to go to the bathroom, and she could have been out of the house in a flash. I know that it is hard because you and your sister have always taken your caring for her so seriously, but you must not blame yourself. It could have happened at any time". She thought to herself that, despite the very tragic circumstances, Maria's mother, and indeed the whole family, had been spared the trauma of a long-drawn-out farewell, which is what Alzheimer's Disease meant to its sufferers – but of course she did not say that.

"The fact is, I cannot get over it. I am not managing to sleep at night, and I think about her all the time. Johanna has done her best to help me too and I do appreciate the fact that she has not blamed me, but the truth is that I still blame myself. I keep asking myself what I can do to make amends somehow for what I did; some way of expiating my big failure to look after my mother."

Greta saw how upset Maria was, so she steered the conversation away from the tragedy and started to tell Maria about what had been going on in her own life. They reminisced too about their last trip together when they visited the Salzkammergut in the Austrian Alps. They had used the lovely, lakeside village of Sankt Wolfgang as a base and each day they had gone on marvelous walks along the lakes and into the mountains of the region. It had been their first trip abroad together and they had both enjoyed it enormously. Both loved walking and experiencing the sights and sounds of nature. They also loved good food and had enjoyed their glass of Grüner Veltliner wine at the end of a day of vigorous exercise. During that week, they had grown quite close, and they had promised themselves that they would do it again sometime soon, but they had never managed because of Maria's commitment to caring for her mother.

Slowly, Maria started to relax and for the first time since the accident, she felt a momentary respite from the tension that tormented her each day and night. She felt then that, while she would always carry the responsibility for her mother's death, she could perhaps resolve her sense of guilt somehow. People came and went, and the bar filled up and then gradually emptied and the two friends continued to chat. Eventually, Maria looked at her watch and realised it was late. She and Greta had been there for several hours and now she needed to get back home to fix something to eat and prepare for bed.

"Listen, Greta. I really must be getting back now. I need to try and catch up on some sleep. Hopefully, after our chat today I will be able to sleep a bit more peacefully than usual."

"I really hope so Maria. It will do you harm if you don't sleep well night after night. It was so good to see you and I want to help you in any way I can." replied Greta, putting her arm round Maria's waist.

"Thanks, Greta for being a true friend. Do let's meet again soon."

And with that, the two friends hugged each other and left the bar to make their way home.

That night, Maria slept better than she had done in some days, and she awoke feeling better able to face the day. While she was at work, Greta popped in to see her and to ask her whether they could meet again after work. Maria consented immediately and they agreed to meet at their favourite bar at six. During the day, she called Chief Inspector Grungo to check whether there had been any developments, but he told her that, regretfully, things were at a standstill because there was so little evidence. She felt her disappointment and anger rise as he said this. Again, she felt hate for the person who had done this, who had struck her mother and had then driven off, leaving her fatally injured and at risk of being struck by another car. She thanked the inspector and once again, urged him to try to find the culprit.

At a quarter to six, she left the office and went to the bar to meet her friend. Greta was already there waiting for her, seated at their usual corner table. They greeted and hugged each other and then called the waiter over to order their drinks. Greta started to tell Maria that she had thought a lot about what they had discussed the day before and she had a plan. Maria knew from experience that Greta always took a situation by the horns and tried to plan a solution to the problem. Greta then explained what she had in mind.

"I thought a lot about what we discussed yesterday, Maria. I think that your feelings of guilt are unjustified, but I can understand that you may be experiencing them. There may be ways in which you can lay these feelings of guilt to rest".

"I wish I could, Greta, but whichever angle I look at it from, it always comes back to the same point of departure – that if I had not been distracted, my mother might still be around".

"I told you yesterday that this could have happened in so many other ways. You are feeling guilt, perhaps, because the reason for your distraction was that, at the time, you were talking with the boyfriend whom your mother did not like."

"Well, yes, maybe that was part of it, but it doesn't change the fact that my being distracted led to my mother's death."

"OK, let's accept that premise, although I don't agree with it. What are you going to do about it? You cannot continue in this way. It will affect your health, both physically and mentally."

"I really don't know, except that I feel that somehow I need to expiate what I see as my big failing, my selfishness, my sin."

"As I said, I thought a lot about our conversation yesterday. I believe you need something that will take you away from your present milieu and from your feelings of guilt; something which could enable you to experience the expiation that you think you need."

"But what…?" asked Maria.

Greta paused for a few moments, and then she said, "How would you feel about going on a pilgrimage? It will be long and hard, and it may help you achieve this sense of expiation or atonement that you feel you need. It will also take you away from Malta for some weeks which, perhaps, you could do with."

"What are you talking about, Greta?"

"Have you ever heard about the Camino to Santiago de Compostela?"

"No, what's that?"

"It's a walk across the whole of Spain, going from the French border to the west coast of Spain. It started way back in the Middle Ages and is still going on today. In the past, many of those who went did it to expiate their sins. Nowadays, lots of people of all kinds do this every year to find peace and solace. How would you feel about that?"

"I don't know. It sounds rather daunting, but …how would it help me?"

"I have a couple of friends who have done it and they tell me that it was one of the greatest experiences of their lives, one that helped them come to terms with a number of issues they were facing at the time."

"But Greta, much as I am used to walking, I have never done anything like this before. My walks – and indeed our own walks together in Austria – have been daylong excursions. How could I even dream of doing something like this?"

"You know, Maria, I would be happy to come with you. Let's do this together! Let me be with you and help you along the way. From what I have heard, I think it would be a great experience, and one that would help you – both of us, actually – to face the challenges that life throws at us."

Greta proceeded to tell Maria all about it. Maria listened with great interest and then spent several minutes thinking to herself. Greta meanwhile went and paid the bill. When she came back, Maria said to her,

"Greta. I will give it some thought over the next few days and we will talk again."

"OK dear, let's do that."

They agreed to meet in a couple of days' time to discuss it further.

When they met again, Maria arrived slightly late and was somewhat breathless. As she walked towards Greta, she noticed that her friend had brought along a number of books and pamphlets. She realised soon enough that they were guidebooks for the pilgrimage, which her friend had mentioned to her. Greta then started to go over it with Maria. She showed her the route through Spain and the cities, towns and villages through which it passed. She explained the history of the pilgrimage and the fact that hundreds of thousands of pilgrims had walked the way to atone for their sins and to find peace. Maria was somewhat sceptical at first, but her friend seemed to be so enthusiastic about the pilgrimage and soon enough, despite herself, Maria started to listen more closely and with greater interest. She thought back to their trip in the Austrian Alps and the great time they had had then, and she considered that, even if it were to be only a re-creation of that wonderful week, it might still help her. Finally, she consented to meet one more time before coming to a decision.

The rest of the week was a very busy time. She and Johanna were in the process of starting to sort out their mother's affairs. It wasn't easy. They realised that their mother's condition must have started to deteriorate well before it became apparent to them. Whereas in the past she had always been highly organised and kept meticulous files on all her financial and legal affairs, it was now clear that in the last few years she had become very erratic and far less organised.

Maria thought to herself what a cruel illness dementia was; it stole upon one so subtly and insidiously, yet at the same time, remorselessly. She met her sister to try to piece together what her mother had done with her few investments, and they tried to establish what commitments her mother had left behind. They started to go through the contents of her laptop. Their mother was a latecomer to the digital world but, unlike many of her contemporaries, she had embraced it with some confidence and enthusiasm. She had been generally able to conduct her affairs using her laptop, without asking for help too often from her more computer-savvy daughters. Apart from the more mundane data, they found that their mother had been keeping a diary since some years back although, in recent months, the entries had tended to be sporadic and quite brief. They read, with tears in their eyes, their mother's description of the death of their father and of her widowhood. 'Perhaps', Maria thought, 'this had been a contributing factor to the deterioration in their mother's mental state'. Even more painful was their dealing with her personal effects, especially her clothes. They associated some of her dresses with particular events that they had shared, and which had a lot of meaning to them both. They went through the old photo albums, which was also very hard, as it brought back so many memories. They agreed to make copies of all the photos to keep a set each, as they did not want to be parted from these memories of their mother and their past.

All this took up a lot of Maria's time, so she didn't think further about Greta's suggestion until she decided to do a bit of research of her own before they met up again. She looked up 'Camino to Santiago de Compostela' on the internet and it brought up a host of entries. As she started to go through them, one thing led to another and several hours passed. She had made some notes as she went along and these led, in turn, to other related topics. By the end of it, she was starting to form a picture of what it was all about, and her friend's suggestion was starting to seem more attractive. Perhaps, it could be just what she was looking for. She was especially attracted to what appeared to be the sense of spirituality that the Camino engendered in many of those who walked it. She had always been a very spiritual person herself and she could perceive how it might help her to find peace in atoning for her failure to protect her mother from harm. She phoned Greta and told her that they should meet again, and they fixed a date for the following evening.

This time, Maria was there first, but Greta arrived soon after. Maria got straight to the point, "I've done some research on the Camino, Greta, and it seems like something that could be helpful. I think I would like to do it, if you are ready to come as well, that is."

"Are you sure, Maria? This is not something you embark on lightly. It can be pretty demanding"

"I think so. I've read a lot about it and it ticks a lot of boxes and it could, perhaps, help me come to terms with what has happened."

"Well, you will need to see for how long you would be able to be away … me too, of course."

"I don't know. I would need to discuss that with Arnold."

"As I will too! Firstly, we need to decide how much of the way we want to walk, and then check this out against the leave that we would be granted."

"Yes. From what I have read, I think that one should try and walk as much as possible the whole way. Of course, that could take four weeks or more."

Suddenly, they were both excited at the prospect of undertaking this challenge together and talked vivaciously for the next couple of hours. They consulted the guidebooks that Greta had brought along and were able to prepare some preliminary plans, even listing the equipment they would need to buy, although they had some of it already from their previous trip. They tentatively decided to start the walk from Pamplona, which was the first major city on the route. They dismissed the idea of starting from Saint-Jean-Pied-de-Port, which is where the 'Camino Frances' was deemed to start, because they were reluctant to have to face what seemed like an extremely gruelling climb up the Pyrenees Mountains on the very first day of their walk. They calculated that the walk from Pamplona to Santiago would take the better part of thirty days.

Chapter 5

James had just finished his breakfast when there was a ring at the door. He checked the video hall porter and asked the caller what he wanted. It was a delivery from Amazon. He opened the door and signed for the package then took it into the kitchen to see what it was, since he was expecting a number of different items he had ordered. This one proved to be the guidebook to the Camino. He leafed through it briefly although he wanted very badly to read it but, since he was expected in the office in half an hour's time, he would have to postpone the pleasure until the evening.

When he arrived at the office, he was totally immersed in his work, as a number of issues which needed his full concentration, had come up. He had to struggle with himself to stay focused, but with Lisa's help, he managed to do so and to tackle the complexities of these issues. His firm had managed to secure some significant consultancy jobs and, up to the time of the accident, he had been so excited about the challenges and the opportunities that these presented. Over the years, he had built up a successful planning-consultancy firm, and this had grown from a couple of helpers to a staff of some thirty people. He had handpicked each and every one of them and felt that he had made the right choice in every case. He was especially pleased with his deputy, Peter. He knew that he could trust him completely and felt great comfort in the thought that, were anything to take him away from work for some time, such as an illness, the business could continue to operate at the same level of efficiency. He was proud of what he had achieved in his professional life but had always felt something of a failure in some aspects of his personal life. Although he had had a number of relationships, none of them had ever lasted. He regretted never having married, and not having children, like many of his friends and contemporaries did. He had no siblings, so he felt he had missed out on that too. Now, to top it all, he felt that he had betrayed a lot of what he thought he stood for – a decent and principled person, a practicing Catholic and a respected member of the community. What would people think of him if they knew the truth of what he had done? More importantly, how could he himself live with the thought of what he had done, something that went against all of his principles, and which he had never imagined himself capable of.

That evening when he got home from work, he sat down to read the guidebook. It was well presented, and had a detailed description of the walk, with each of the various stages listed, together with the distance and the change in elevation, thus giving an indication of the difficulty of each stage. It also contained a wealth of detail about the accommodation along the way. This ranged from very basic hostels called *albergues,* to pensions and even hotels, including some luxurious ones like the Paradores, state-owned hotels that the Spanish Government had set up in a variety of heritage buildings such as palaces, monasteries, castles and so on. The guide also contained the raison d'être of the Camino, and its detailed history from the earliest beginnings to the present day. It also provided a great deal of information about the more mundane details, such as what clothing and equipment was needed, and how to get to the start point. James learnt that each pilgrim was expected to collect a pilgrim's passport called a *Credencial* from the Pilgrims' Office at the start point, and this was to be stamped at every stop on the way. Upon arrival at Santiago de Compostela, the pilgrim would present his *Credencial* to the Pilgrims' Office there to be given the *Compostela*, a certificate confirming that the pilgrim had walked 'The Way'. He saw some illustrations of this in the guidebook. It was a beautiful document on parchment and written in Latin, reminding him of the illuminated manuscripts of the early Middle Ages.

He understood that one could start at almost any point along the way. The only proviso was that, if one wanted to obtain a *Compostela* at the end of it, one had to walk at least one hundred kilometres. The 'Camino Frances' began at the small *Basses-Pyrénées* village of Saint-Jean-Pied-de-Port, just across the Franco-Spanish border. From there it crossed the Pyrenees into Spain and then traversed the whole of Northern Spain up to Santiago de Compostela – the city of his namesake saint. From the guidebook, he reckoned that it would take some thirty-three days to complete. He had never been one to take shortcuts, therefore he decided that, if he was going to do this, it would have to be all or nothing. He made a few cursory notes about what he had read, including the compilation of a list of equipment and clothing he would need.

It seemed like something that could initially distract him, and take him away from his present predicament, at least for a time. More importantly, it would be something that perhaps could provide him with a way of atoning and achieving forgiveness for what he had done, so he started to plan it actively. The first thing he had to do was to ascertain whether he could possibly leave the office for four weeks or more, therefore he scheduled a meeting with Peter for the next morning in his office. James introduced the subject by telling Peter that he was going through a bad patch, jokingly referring to a possible early onset of male menopause, then changing his tone to a more serious one, saying that it was just a difficult period. He told Peter that, in a nutshell, he needed to get away for a time. Lisa had already voiced her worries about James to Peter, so he was not too surprised when James said this. He also felt concern for his employer and colleague.

"James. Is there anything you need to talk to me about? I know how tough these years have been for you, building up the firm. I can understand that one can suffer from an element of burnout," he asked, with obvious concern.

"I don't think it's that. It's just that a series of things have been happening to me and have accumulated. I guess I just need to take a bit of a break," said James, evading the question.

"Well, I can understand that. When was the last time that you took a break?"

"Aside from the odd long weekend, it must be a few years since my last holiday, which was only for a week, anyway."

"Why don't you take one then?"

"That's exactly what I wanted to talk to you about, Peter. I think that I really need a break to get away from things for a few weeks, as otherwise I feel I am going to crack. Would you be able to help me by taking over while I am away?"

"I guess I could. We will need to hold a few meetings for you to bring me up to speed on the projects you have been handling directly. I can deal with the rest, as well as all the admin issues. When were you planning to do this and for how long will you be away?"

"Well, I was thinking of taking four to five weeks in a few weeks' time. That should give us enough time to have things in order and for me to give you a proper handing over."

"Listen, James. I think you both need and deserve this break. I will take care of things while you are away. It will be no problem so long as we go over things before you leave."

"Thanks, Peter. I really appreciate this. I hope to come back feeling totally renewed."

"Have you any idea where you are going?"

James was still reluctant to disclose his plans to anyone, so he replied that he was still mulling over a number of options. He thanked Peter once again and they agreed to start their coordination meetings within the next couple of days, after which Peter went back to his own office. James realised that the whole project was starting to become more realistic and immediate. He knew that, apart from his work issues, he would also need to organise a few things at home if he were going to be away for so long. That should not prove to be too difficult as he had no family, but he would have to ask his housekeeper, Martha, to take a few weeks off, something he was sure she would not be averse to, especially as she too had not taken a decent holiday in some time. Sure enough, she accepted readily when he told her about it the next day.

Then he started planning his walk in earnest. He had already decided that he would start from Saint-Jean-Pied-de-

Port, so he started by trying to work out how best to get there. There were several options. He could fly to Marseille and then take a train, or he could fly to Paris and then take a flight to Biarritz, on the Bay of Biscay. From there, it was a much shorter train journey to Saint-Jean-Pied-de-Port. He decided to postpone the choice for the moment.

Next, he started to list all the clothing and equipment he would need. Although he walked regularly, he had never been on a trek as long as this one would be. His guidebook proposed a list, and he wondered from where it would be best to buy the equipment. He would have to start practically from scratch. He would need a medium-sized rucksack, a sleeping bag and an inflatable pillow, a quick-dry towel and a head-mounted, miner's torch, which would leave his hands free. Most importantly of all, he needed to get a good pair of hiking boots and walking poles. He read that he should try and limit the weight of his backpack to ten percent of his body weight, which at first, seemed difficult. Next, he looked at the clothes. He needed to have three sets of everything so, assuming he could only wash his clothes every other day, he would always have one set of clean clothes.

He looked for, and found, a good hat. He sought a good store that could provide all his requirements. As he surfed the internet, he came across a French organisation, called *Aux Vieux Campeurs*. He was fascinated when he saw that they had some thirty different shops within the same neighbourhood in Paris. Each shop specialised in some branch of sports or outdoor living, with several of them being dedicated to hiking and camping. He browsed through their products and realised that they would be able to supply his every need, and more. That decided his travelling options. He would fly to Paris, buy all his equipment there, and then fly down to Biarritz. The only exception would be his boots. He knew from painful experience that one had to break in one's boots before embarking on any major walk, so he decided to buy them locally. Within a couple of days, he had booked his flights and his hotel in Paris and made all the remaining arrangements. All that was left now was to wait for the date of his departure, set for the 17th May, while preparing himself physically, emotionally and spiritually for the walk.

The next few weeks were a gruelling time for James. He had set himself a training regime during the relatively short time left prior to his departure. He was still getting too little sleep at night, and then waking up very early in the morning, as he was trying to fit his training in before going to work. He would try and walk several kilometres, trying to include some substantial hill climbs when he could. On the weekends, he would go for longer walks, often for fifteen or twenty kilometres, in the countryside.

Slowly, he built up stamina and, despite his tiredness through lack of sleep, he started to feel more confident about being able to complete the walk. His sessions with Peter were going well and he felt quite certain that his friend would hold the fort in his absence. His sense of guilt had not abated much and he still felt great shame when he thought about that night. Occasionally, the emotional pain he would experience could be excruciating and it left him with an extremely low sense of self-esteem. He, who had always believed himself to be a good, upright and law-abiding member of society, now felt like a pariah, except that only he knew that, and for the moment, that is how it would have to remain. He determined that he would not talk to anyone about what was really troubling him, except for Father Joe. When he remembered his confession, he thought that he should perhaps tell him what he had decided to do and ask him for his opinion. So, he called him up and asked for another appointment.

When they met, his friend asked him how he was feeling and whether he had told anyone about what had happened, and whether he had decided to confess his guilt to the authorities. James admitted that he had not, but he then told him about his decision to walk the Camino, and what had prompted him to do this. He explained that he hoped this would enable him to atone for his wrongdoing and thus, perhaps, feel that he might obtain true forgiveness. Father Joe told him that prayer and penitence would help him, and that he should make the most of the time he would be alone to meditate about his life, and the direction it had taken.

Chapter 6

Maria called Arnold the next day and asked him for a meeting. He greeted her with a lot of warmth, perhaps even more than usual, as had been the case since her mother's death. She started to tell him about what she had been going through but then decided to come straight to the point.

"Arnold, I really feel that I need to take a good break. I have been finding it difficult to concentrate on my work and I need some space to mourn. I was thinking of a change of scene."

"What do you mean?" he replied, anxiously, thinking that she might be quitting her job.

"I need to get away from Malta and do something that will help me get out of the frame of mind I am in, and to come to terms with my mother's death. I believe I may have found a way how to do this. Greta has offered to come with me. I realise this would mean that you would be having to make do with two members of staff on leave at the same time, but I can arrange to hand over a large part of my work to William. He has been great these last months, ever since you appointed him as my assistant."

"How long were you thinking of?"

"Four to four and a half weeks," she replied, hesitantly.

"Whoa, Maria!" he exclaimed. He had been expecting her to say a week or two, at most. "That's a pretty long break. I would really like to help you on this, if I can, but give me till tomorrow to see if I could handle your combined absences for so long."

She nodded her assent, and on that note, they parted.

Maria was on tenterhooks for the rest of the day. She called Greta to ask her whether she too had been to see Arnold, and she replied that she had, and that he had told her pretty much the same thing. There was now nothing for it but to wait till the next day for his response. She did not have to wait too long. He .called her before the lunch-break and she went over to his office. In his typically kind and avuncular way, he told her that he had it all worked out and it would be no problem for them both to take their leave. All he requested was that they made sure they returned, as he could not possibly do without them, and he added as an afterthought that he wanted to hear all about their travels.

"Where are you planning to go?" he asked her.

"We're going to Spain. Greta told me about this amazing pilgrimage there which I believe is what I, perhaps both of us, need at this point in our lives. You know, contact with nature, which is so lacking here, time to meditate, a change of scene, meeting new people and returning to basics."

"You must be referring to the Camino, then," said Arnold. "I have heard a good bit about it myself from some friends who walked it last year. They were over the moon about it too, although they did say that it was pretty tough going at times. Are you sure that this is what you want?"

"I think so, yes."

"Well, good luck with it but make sure that you come back in one piece," he said smilingly, as he saw her out of his office.

That evening, Greta came to Maria's place to carry on planning, and they fixed their date of departure. They would take the early morning flight to Madrid and then a train to Pamplona. The train journey would be about three and a half hours long, so they expected to be in Pamplona by four in the afternoon. That meant they would have to spend the night there and start walking the following morning.

They looked up places to stay there and found out a bit about the city. It was well known for the running of the bulls, which took place once a year on some feast day or other. The bulls were made to run through the main street of the city, together with whoever was mad enough to run with them. Maria remembered reading Hemingway's 'The Sun Also Rises', in which he described this unique event. She thought to herself that it would be a strange way to begin her introduction to Spain, a country she had never visited before. From there, they reckoned that they would need some thirty days to reach Santiago, assuming they walked every day.

They looked at the accommodation featured in the guidebooks, the so-called *albergues*. These were pilgrims' hostels, and while they seemed quite basic, it seemed that they were an essential part of the Camino experience. It was here that pilgrims met at the end of the day, either with others they had walked with during the day, or with new acquaintances. It was here that pilgrims would dine together in the refectories or knock together a meal for themselves in the kitchen. All this served to enhance the great sense of camaraderie that the Camino generated, and it seemed that most pilgrims preferred to stay in them for that very reason.

That night, they managed to plan every, last detail as far as they could.

In the following days, they started to prepare themselves physically for the walk. They started with relatively short seven to ten-kilometre walks, then built these up to fifteen and twenty kilometres on the weekends. Their fitness level increased, and they found they were able to take longer walks in their stride quite easily. Then they started to carry a rucksack, which they loaded with books to replicate the weight they expected to be carrying. That made it harder, of course, but after a few more days of it, that too became easier, especially when they used their walking poles.

Maria was still suffering, particularly at night. She would wake up several times and then find it hard to go back to sleep, as images of the night of her mother's death flooded back. Although, in the last few days, the excitement about the Camino and the distraction it brought with it had helped her to some extent, her sense of guilt and the pain caused by her loss were still very much present. She still found it difficult to talk about it, except with her sister and with Greta. With everyone else, she clammed up and would reply in monosyllables to their, often well-meaning, questions.

She had not seen as much of Johanna in the last few days as she had in the immediate aftermath of her mother's death. Johanna had a family to look after and, while she cared for her sister a lot, her first commitment was to her husband and children. The latter were going through a difficult time at school and they needed their mother's help every day.

Maria started to count the days until their departure, hoping that this would bring about a much-needed respite or, better still, a resolution of her feelings. There was not much longer to wait now.

Chapter 7

On the eve of his departure, James went to bed early. Everything was ready for the morrow. He had ticked off all the tasks on his list one by one and was now ready to go. He found it hard to fall asleep. This time it was not so much through his usual feelings of guilt and disquiet, but rather due to the excitement of the journey into the unknown that was about to start. Finally, he managed to drop off.

He woke up well before his alarm rang and was ready in good time. His taxi was punctual, collected him and took him to the airport without any problems.

The flight was full of French tourists returning home, as well as a few Maltese, but no one he knew. Much as he loved flying, he hated the prelude to it – the security checks and the sometimes-long waits at airports, but now that he was sitting in the plane and waiting to take off, he felt the familiar excitement he experienced every time he boarded a plane. They left on time and the flight to Paris was quite uneventful. When he arrived, he took a taxi straight to his hotel in the *Rue de Rivoli*. After he had unpacked a few basics from his rucksack, he set off to the *Rive Gauche* and the galaxy of shops that formed *Les Vieux Campeurs*. He found it without any difficulty. It was fascinating to see this collection of shops, none of them particularly large but, all having the same shop-front, they were very clearly identifiable. Sometimes there were two or three shops in the same street but all of them were within two hundred metres of each other. He found the one that sold hiking gear and was struck by the enormous range of products available. He would never have found anything remotely like this in Malta, and probably not even in London!

He started by selecting a 60-litre rucksack with a large number of different zipped compartments, which would make the organising of his gear so much easier. He then bought two pairs of cotton hiking socks, two moisture-wicking shirts, one quick dry, transformable pair of trousers, and another waterproof one. He was already wearing the third set of clothes, which he had bought in Malta, and worn for his flight. Next, he chose a bright red, light anorak. He thought that this would be far more visible to rescuers in the event that he were to have any mishaps along the way. He also bought a poncho that could fold up into a very small space. The weather along the Camino could be quite rainy, especially in the final stage in Galicia, which was reputedly often very wet. He packed all his gear into the rucksack and hefted it onto his shoulders. It felt quite manageable.

By the time he had finished, the afternoon had turned into early evening, but it was still sunny as the days were getting longer, so he decided to take a walk before heading back to his hotel. He walked towards the Seine and crossed one of the bridges to the Île de la Cité . He wanted to visit Notre-Dame cathedral but knew it was still closed to visitors after the fire. However, he had not been to Paris since then and he wanted to see for himself what works had been done so far.

The square in front of the cathedral was, as always, thronged with people. There were tourists taking photos and many families sitting on the benches. He remembered the last time he had been there. He had attended a high Mass on a Sunday morning, which was an unforgettable experience: the great soaring height of the cathedral reaching upwards, the wonderful stained-glass windows, the celebrants intoning the prayers of the Mass and a heavenly choir filling the cavernous space with ethereal music. He wondered how much of the stained glass had survived the fire, and whether all the damage caused could be repaired with the cathedral being restored completely to its erstwhile glory. Hopefully, the repairs would be completed successfully and quickly, so that the cathedral could open its doors, once more, to the people of France and of the world. He spent some time deep in these thoughts and then moved onwards to his hotel as he wanted to have a quiet evening, read his guidebook once again and have an early night. His flight to Biarritz was due to leave Orly early the next morning.

He awoke before sunrise and, after a quick breakfast at the hotel, he got a taxi to the airport. He managed to persuade the clerk at the check-in counter to allow him to take his rucksack and walking poles on as cabin luggage. The flight was only half-full, and he was able to get a window seat with no difficulty. It was a brilliant day, sunny with not a cloud in the sky. As they flew towards Biarritz, they overflew the Bordeaux region, and he was able to pick out the Medoc and the Entre Deux Mers areas quite easily. James was a keen, and fairly-knowledgeable, wine enthusiast, and he knew these regions well from what he had read, although he had yet to visit them. Soon after, they landed in Biarritz and he hailed a taxi outside the airport and asked to be taken to the railway station at nearby Bayonne, from where he would take the train to Saint-Jean-Pied-de-Port. There were several backpackers waiting at the station, and he assumed that they were probably pilgrims like himself. The train journey lasted just over an hour. The railway passed through the very picturesque valley of the river Nive and, as they neared their destination, James caught glimpses of the snow-capped Pyrenees in the distance.

He took some time to observe the occupants of his carriage. There were what seemed like some locals, an elderly couple, a younger family with two rather boisterous children and a business traveller. The remaining occupants were clearly pilgrims like himself – two or three different groups all talking animatedly in their respective languages – Italian, German and American English. When they finally reached St Jean, and he got off the train, a couple of Australian ladies walked up to him and asked him to take their photo with the station as a backdrop. He walked through the little town and found his hostel without difficulty, since he had a pretty good idea of the layout of the town from his preparations.

After he checked in, he went to the Pilgrims' Office in the Rue de la Citadelle to collect his 'Pilgrim's Passport'. In Spanish, this was called a Credencial and it was a foldout document, which certified that the bearer was a pilgrim. It would have to be stamped each day along the route. He got his first stamp there, in the Pilgrims' Office, after having to wait in a queue for some time. As it was still the early afternoon, he decided to explore the town and soon realised how very attractive it was. It was built on both sides of the river Nive and it was dominated by the citadel on the hill above it. It had been a walled town and parts of the old fortifications still existed, including the different gates, one of which, the Porte d'Espagne, was the one he would walk out through the next day to start the Camino.

That evening, he went to Mass at the church of Notre Dame in the centre of the town. There were very few people attending. As the service was ending, one of the people next to him motioned him to step forward to the altar. She explained that the priest had just called for any pilgrims in the church to present themselves to be blessed. He followed her instructions and noticed that two young people did the same. They stood together in front of the priest, who blessed them while saying a prayer. James could not speak French, but he knew enough to understand that the priest was blessing them and wishing them Godspeed on their pilgrimage. He finally asked them to pray for those present in the church when they reached faraway Santiago. As he walked out of the church, he spoke to the other two pilgrims, who were Peter, a young American, and Gina, an even younger New Zealander. Both said that they were starting the Camino the next day and, as they wished each other goodbye, they hoped that they might meet the next day.

Earlier in the day, James had spotted a little restaurant with a terrace perched over the river and had already decided that he would dine there, so he set off to it. He ordered fresh trout served with an almond sauce, quite an unusual pairing, but it was excellent, washing it down with a glass of the local Basque wine. As he dined alone, he again started to think about what he was going to undertake. He realised that his need for repentance and atonement was only a part of the raison d'être for his decision to walk the Camino. Part of it had also been the allure of the challenge, a challenge to his stamina and courage, and the promise that it held in terms of experiencing the wonderful countryside, the culture, and the people he would meet along the way. The idea of a very long walk, which never turns back on itself but moves inexorably on in one direction to its final destination seemed to him a bit like life in microcosm. He was not especially religious, although he did practise his faith, nor did he feel any special affinity to his namesake saint, yet the idea of a spiritual and religious experience appealed to him, especially in his present circumstances of suffering from extreme feelings of guilt and self-recrimination.

He hoped that he would find solace and some resolution of his condition and ultimately, forgiveness. Despite the slight respite in his torments thanks to the distraction created by his need to plan and organise things for the walk, he still had difficulty in sleeping and often spent hours awake at night, tossing and turning and trying hard to block the images that presented themselves, out of his mind. However, that night he did manage to sleep a bit better, possibly through sheer exhaustion.

When he awoke the next morning, he looked out of the window. Although it was still very early, he could see that it was going to be a brilliant day. There was not a cloud in the sky and a gentle breeze wafted through the trees. He was all set to start, so he left the hostel and set off towards the Porte D'Espagne, and whatever lay beyond. The town was still very quiet and, as he walked through the cobbled streets, he felt excited, but also apprehensive. The route of the Camino was marked with a series of yellow arrows painted on walls, utility poles or traffic signs, or actual waymarks, which featured a yellow conch shell on a blue background, the symbol of the Camino. He had read that there were two options to cross the Pyrenees. The easier, and less demanding, one went through the valley of Valcarlos, while the Route Napoleon, the much harder but also far more spectacular one, went over the top of a high pass. Whichever of the two he would take depended mainly on the weather, since the Route Napoleon could be dangerous in bad weather.

When he got to the fork in the road where the two routes parted company, he did not hesitate for one moment, and chose the harder option over the mountains. It did not take him long to realise just how hard it was going to be. The road started to climb upwards at a steep gradient just after leaving St Jean. Despite the difficulty, he felt quite exhilarated at having started and as he saw other pilgrims ahead of him, he felt a certain reassurance. The walk up to the village of Hunto was steep, but what came after that was something else altogether. The path switch-backed up the mountain at a punishing gradient for several hundred metres until it reached the Auberge D'Orisson, which was the only stop along that part of the route where one could get something to eat or drink. After the grueling climb he had just completed, he stopped for a snack and a coffee. He found a seat on the terrace with a spectacular view of the mountains. After a few minutes, Peter arrived and joined him, and they exchanged notes about the walk so far. Soon it was time to press on.

In a short while, the climb became extremely demanding until he reached a popular shrine high up on the mountain called the Vierge de Biakorri. There, a statue of the Virgin stood atop a pile of rocks, on which many flowers and votive offerings had been laid. Immediately to one side, the ground dropped away steeply into a valley, the floor of which was some nine hundred metres below. James had always had a fear of heights but in the sheer exhilaration of the moment, he was able to look down and around with equanimity. The views were spectacular, with green hills plunging into the valley depths while picturesque little villages clung to the slopes or nestled in the valley below. In the distance, there was the snow-covered peak of the Pic d'Orisson, which he would be approaching soon. A remorseless slope followed and the tiredness and pain in his legs was now excruciating. Every three minutes, he was having to stop for a minute or more, to rest. His legs were screaming at him to stop but he knew he had to go on. After an hour or so, the path levelled out a bit and he crossed the border into Spain, but then the path started to rise again until finally, he reached the top of the pass. His sense of relief when he got there was almost indescribable. He stopped to eat a sandwich and looked down into the valley far below, and forward to his destination of the day, the small Spanish village of Roncesvalles.

Chapter 8

Three days before their intended departure to Madrid, Maria and Greta had completed all their preparations, and booked their flights and their first night in a hotel. All that remained for them to do was to pack their rucksacks. They had both been working overtime to make sure that they handed over all their work to their respective replacements and this seemed to be going well. Arnold was starting to feel reassured that he would be able to do without two of his key staff members for a few weeks. Maria had also spent time with Johanna, sorting out their mother's affairs. Their mother had left a will and the two sisters were equal beneficiaries. They had no problem agreeing on how they would share the estate and the personal effects of their mother, even though each one had particular affinities to certain of their mother's things, which brought back individual memories.

Maria had discussed her forthcoming trip with Johanna, who had expressed some reservations, mainly that she was worried about Maria's ability to handle the rigours of such a long and demanding walk. She also expressed concern about the fact that she would be meeting all sorts of people along the way, some decent and others, maybe, not so decent. She still felt protective towards her younger sister, but she conceded that Maria would not be walking on her own. The training that she and Greta had put in over the last weeks had made them fitter and they were both looking the better for it. They had both lost some weight and they were feeling physically on top of the world, although Maria was still suffering from lack of sleep.

When she got home from work, Maria was checking the local weather in Pamplona, just as she had done every evening for the past week, when Greta called.

"Hi, Maria. It's me, Greta."

"Hi Greta. I was about to call you. I have just been going over the start of our trip in my mind and I was sure that we had it all planned out but then I thought that …"

"Maria, Maria! Sorry to interrupt you, but there's a problem. Some bad news."

"What's the matter? What happened?"

"It's John. He has been diagnosed with cancer, and…"

"Eva's John?" Maria interrupted, assuming that Greta must be referring to her brother-in-law, rather than her own ex-boyfriend.

"Yes. He'll be going into hospital next week for chemo and Eva will need help with the children. With their exams coming up soon, they'll need constant ferrying here and there. They haven't told the children yet, but they're both worried sick. Eva needs me, Maria. She's barely holding it together as it is."

"Poor Eva!"

"Yes. It's terrible. But unfortunately, there's no way I can go with you."

"Of course not! I understand," Maria said, knowing that Eva had no one else. Both their parents were long since dead and there were no other siblings. "I am really sorry, Greta. Truly. It must be so terrible for your sister. They are both still quite young."

"Yes, they are. This is all so unexpected! I feel bad for you, Maria. I really wanted us to do it together, but it's not going to be possible, I'm so sorry," Greta said, her voice breaking.

"Greta, you must not feel bad on my account. Your sister needs help, and you are the only relative she has. So, help her, you must!"

After they had hung up, Maria went up to her room to think about the news she had just received. Now, she would have to decide whether to go ahead on her own, or cancel at this late stage, hoping to get refunds on flights and hotels. She thought long and hard, reaching no conclusion and finally decided to sleep on it. She had learnt from experience that one's subconscious did amazing things at night. She had often, in the course of her work, reached a brick wall during the day but, having assimilated all the facts of a problem she was trying to solve, her mind would often throw up a solution on its own, the next morning.

Her sleep was disturbed, and she had many dreams where reality and fantasy mixed in a strange way. She awoke still feeling disturbed but, as half expected, her brain had indeed been working overtime at night, and it was clear to her that she should proceed with her plans. When she tried to rationalise her decision, it hinged essentially on the realisation that she needed this break now, not at some later stage. She needed to come to terms with her demons immediately. She thought it through another couple of times but remained unchanged in her resolve to go ahead. After a while, she called up Greta and told her about her decision. Her friend told her that she fully understood, agreeing with Maria that she needed to take this break in her life sooner rather than later. She wished Maria well, told her to take a lot of photos, and to keep in touch while she was in Spain.

This change in plans did not affect her arrangements. It was more a case of coming to terms with the idea that she would be walking alone for four weeks or more. However, from what she had read, she knew that the Camino Frances was a very popular route, and that there would be very many pilgrims walking the way, making it highly likely that she would meet people with whom she could walk. Still, she started trying to psyche herself up for the change. She discussed the change of plan with Johanna who, at first, was somewhat alarmed at the thought of her younger sister going off into the 'wilds of Spain' for four weeks on her own. As Maria told her more about it, she started to relax until finally she told her to go ahead but to be careful with whom she walked and hung around with, telling her to call often, preferably every day.

On the eve of her departure, Maria went to the cemetery and placed some flowers on her mother's grave. She stood there for some time thinking about her mother's life, and her untimely death for which she felt responsible. She prayed to her mother to look after her, sensing the irony that she herself had not looked after her mother well enough. As she communed silently with her mother, she thought about what she was about to embark on and prayed that it would assuage her feelings of guilt and bring her inner peace. As she walked down the tree-lined avenue of the cemetery and back to the entrance, the sun was already setting, and it was starting to get dark. She fixed herself a light dinner when she got home, and then tucked herself into bed.

She slept deeply and uninterruptedly for the first time in weeks, and she only woke up when her alarm clock rang. She jumped out of bed and got herself ready. Johanna had offered, very kindly, to take her to the airport and she was ready waiting at the door with her rucksack on her back when her sister drove up. Although it was only just past dawn and the sun had not arisen yet, she could see that it was going to be a beautiful day, which put her in a good frame of mind. When they got to the airport, they got out of the car and Johanna hugged Maria tightly, saying with an impish smile, "Please make sure you come back in one piece."

"I shall, Johanna, but you can still say the odd prayer for me, if you want to."

"Listen, sis, joking apart, look after yourself and stay in touch. I would love to know what you are doing and, if you need anything, call me straight away."

Maria walked into the very busy terminal and up to the check-in counter for Madrid. There was a long queue of mainly Spanish tourists who were returning home. She listened to them talk. Maria did not speak Spanish but spoke Italian and was therefore able to understand a bit of what they were saying. At the same time, she realised that there was a lot of what they said which she did not follow at all. Apart from the fact that many of the words were unfamiliar and quite unlike Italian, they all spoke so fast. She hoped that she would not have a problem communicating with the locals in Spain, especially in the smaller villages along the Camino, where presumably few, if any, of the people spoke English. She felt rather self-conscious in her hiking gear as some of the young Spanish students around looked at her with evident curiosity. Her dress was so different from her usual business attire, and she was suddenly struck again by how different her life would be over the next four or five weeks.

The flight to Madrid took a very different route to what she had imagined. Glancing out of the window, she noticed that sometime after leaving the Maltese Islands, they were flying over a vast area of land, which was neither Sicily nor Sardinia. She realised that it must be the North of Africa and she was somewhat bemused by this as she had imagined that they would have to fly in a north westerly direction to get to Madrid – so what were they doing flying south to Africa? Then she understood that they must have been following a Great Circle route taking them over Tunisia, and part of Algeria.

They landed in Madrid and, as she walked through the airport, she was quite impressed by what she saw. It was a very elegant building and structurally daring, but she did not have time to take it in. She needed to get to the railway station in central Madrid to catch her train to Pamplona. She had around two hours left so she needed to hurry, since it was all new to her and she was not sure how long it would take her to get there. The taxi driver who drove her into the city centre started chatting with her in rather broken English and asked her what she was planning to do in Spain.

He seemed to be an amiable fellow and good looking, to boot, so she responded graciously to his question and told him what she had in mind. He did not seem to be surprised because many pilgrims passed through Madrid on their way to one of the many starting points of the Camino. He told her that his brother had walked it for the first time some years earlier and he had become so thoroughly addicted that he had been back every year since and sometimes even twice in one year. Then she asked him whether he himself had done it. He replied in rather broken English, "No *señora*. Unfortunately, I no can do it. I have to work every day to earn my living. Perhaps, when I am more old, I will try."

"You have something to look forward to then, but you live in a beautiful city in the meantime," she replied, as she glanced out of the window at the wide avenues, monumental buildings and gardens of central Madrid.

At that, he looked back for a shade too long, regaling her with a big smile.

He dropped her off at Atocha Station in central Madrid, and she went straight up to the gate, since she had bought her train ticket online. The train was full already and it left bang on time, so she did not have long to wait. The countryside they passed through was beautiful and she spent a good bit of time looking out of the window. She also took time to observe the occupants of her carriage, trying to guess their occupations, and the sort of people they were. She had been a great fan of Arthur Conan Doyle in her younger years and had read all the Sherlock Holmes books. She loved the way that the first part of the story was almost always a piece of very deft detective work where Holmes would recognise so many characteristics of a person he happened to be observing from little signs, such as a worn-out pair of shoes, calloused fingers, an unusual accent and so on. From these, he would paint an almost complete and accurate picture of the person. Maria loved doing this too. There was a twenty-something-year old, gum-chewing man with a ponytail carrying a guitar, a middle-aged lady in a business suit tapping away frenziedly on a laptop, and an old gentleman who was so distinguished-looking and formidable that she almost looked for medals on his chest. To occupy her time, she thought up stories to fit each person. By the end of the journey, she almost started to feel that she had known these people all her life. Their journey took them through the city of Logroño, which was the capital city of the province of *La Rioja*, and she knew that this was one of the stops on the Camino that she would be walking through in a few days' time.

She arrived in Pamplona in the late afternoon and took a taxi straight to her hotel. On her first night, she had decided to enjoy the comfort of a hotel before starting to use the hostel accommodation provided by the *albergues.* Her hotel was in the *Calle Nueva*, in the heart of the historic centre. After she checked in, she went for a walk around the city. First, she went to the *Oficina de Peregrinos*, the Pilgrims' Office, to collect her pilgrim's passport. She had it stamped, then she carried on walking round the centre.

Pamplona had once been a walled city, but new buildings had spilled outside the old walls. It struck her then that, impressive as the fortifications were, they were diminutive in comparison with the fortifications of Valletta, but then, the Knights of St John had had access to the greatest military engineers of the time, and to almost endless sources of funds. Nevertheless, she enjoyed her walk around the city. At one stage, she went to one of the countless bars and tapas places to have a snack and a glass of the local Basque wine and asked the waiter where and when the running of the bulls would be held.

"*Señora*, it is held during the feast of San Fermín, between the sixth and the fourteenth of July. The bulls are released from one end of the *Casco Historico*, they run along the *Calle de San Domingo* up to the *Plaza de Toros*, which is the bullring. You must come one day and watch it. It is an amazing experience," he explained.

"Yes. Perhaps I will. Does one need to book well ahead to find a hotel?"

"Oh yes, *señora*! You need to book many months before because so many people come at that time."

She was sitting at a table outside in the Plaza Mayor, and again she looked at the people around her. Most were clearly citizens who were taking their tapas and drinks before going on to supper. There were also quite a few tourists and, judging by their garb, a few pilgrims like herself. Some of them looked like they had been walking for many days. Their clothes were stained and tired, their boots looked like they were about to split at the seams, and yet the persons themselves exhibited so much enthusiasm and bonhomie.

There were a number of groups, large and small, all having a great time and talking excitedly about their day's exploits. She wished she could join in and tell them that she was a pilgrim like them, but she felt shy. She noticed that there was a great deal of activity around the bar counter inside the bar itself and, when she had finished her drinks and tapas, she went in to have a look. There was a lavish display of tapas on the bar counter, and the patrons were sampling different ones. She asked what was going on and the barman replied that they had a festival of *Pinchos*, which is what tapas were called there. Each bar in the city produced a plethora of different *pinchos,* all competing with one another to be voted the best. Apparently, this was judged by the number of paper napkins there were at the foot of the bar. She could not understand this, so she pressed the barman further,

"What do you mean? Why would the number of napkins that people have thrown away mean anything?"

"*Señora*", he replied, "when we serve *pinchos,* we always provide a paper napkin. The custom here is for people to throw it away on the floor when they have finished eating. The more paper napkins there are at the foot of the bar, the more popular the *pinchos*, and the bar, are."

As she heard this, she thought to herself that this was indeed a strange way of deciding on the winner, but thought it rather quaint, albeit untidy.

She decided to return to her hotel and have an early night, having had such a long day, and with her starting the Camino in the morning. As she lay in bed, she thought about the next day. On the one hand, she felt ready to start her walk, but on the other, she was having misgivings about the unknown, and doubts about her ability to cope with the physical and emotional challenges involved.

She awoke feeling very keyed up and was soon on her way. She picked up the yellow arrows that marked the Camino and followed them out of the city. Soon, she was out of Pamplona and into the countryside. In the distance, she could see a high ridge with a large number of wind turbines at the top. She had always thought of them as quite intrusive on the landscape and yet these looked weirdly beautiful. The scenery was lovely, with huge seas of corn rippling in a wave-like motion in the wind alternating with whole fields of yellow rapeseed and the dark green of the trees. Above it all, was a clear blue sky, which was set off by the few white clouds. She came across a few other pilgrims along the way and they exchanged greetings with her, wishing her "*Buen Camino*", the universal greeting all along 'The Way'. She pressed on towards the distant ridge and soon the path started to climb inexorably upwards. It was her first experience of a really stiff climb, but she pushed herself on and soon reached the top of the ridge known as the *Alto del Perdon*. She knew enough to understand that this meant the 'hill of forgiveness' and wondered whether there was any significance for her in this. Perhaps, having to climb that difficult slope was some small atonement for the sins one had committed. She was certainly out of breath and felt she needed to stop and rest, while admiring the spectacular view.

There was a metal sculpture nearby, depicting a group of pilgrims, which struck her as particularly appropriate. She had only had a coffee and a croissant for breakfast at the hotel, so she stopped at the next village for a light lunch. There was a large group of pilgrims sitting outside the restaurant, which was offering a special menu for pilgrims at only nine euros. She sat at one of the tables, and soon enough a young couple came and sat next to her, and they started chatting. They were Brazilian and had been married for a few years, but still childless. They confided in her that they were doing this in the hope of being blessed with a large family. She thought to herself that this was a sweet, but rather naïve, hope. She spoke to several other people who were there, and all talked very openly about themselves. She started to realise how all the usual social taboos and restrictions simply did not exist there.

She found it difficult to get going again after lunch because she had already started to unwind and had to force herself to carry on. She still had some distance to walk to her planned destination of *Puente la Reina*. On the way, she took a little detour to the small church of *Santa Maria de Eunate*, which was featured in her guidebook. It was an interesting, octagonal building with a freestanding porch running around the exterior of the church. She spent some time there imbibing the very special atmosphere of the place, until she realised that she should press on to her destination.

She arrived there an hour later and went straight to the *albergue* and asked for a bed. Fortunately, they had one and she was shown to the dormitory. There were some fifty beds, in double-bunk form. The room was not particularly large, and the bunks were crammed together with only a narrow passageway between them, and with no provision for a wardrobe or hanging space of any kind. Next, she inspected the bathroom facilities. They were quite basic, with only two or three showers and loos for fifty-odd people. This was a far cry from what she was used to when travelling, but it was what the Camino was all about, going back to basics and denying herself but, at the same time, experiencing the feeling of camaraderie that came from sharing hardship with other, like-minded pilgrims.

Supper was served early. There was a pilgrims' menu, which was actually quite good. She enjoyed the *cordero asado* (roast lamb) and the *patatas bravas* (potatoes in a spicy sauce), washed down with a glass or two of Rioja. There was a lively atmosphere at the table. All were in high spirits, talking animatedly about their experiences of the day and their plans for the morrow. There must have been pilgrims from seven or more different countries and, once again, she found herself being pleasantly surprised at how all the usual social and national barriers broke down and people conversed together so readily. After a few glasses of Rioja, and a long day on the road, Maria was ready for bed.

Chapter 9

As he entered the cobbled streets of Roncesvalles, he realised that the village was very small, but it was also very attractive. There was an exquisite Gothic-style church, a large *albergue*, a small hotel and a few houses. He checked into the *albergue* and got his *credencial* stamped. There were many pilgrims milling about and all seemed to be in very high spirits. The village was, and always had been, an important way station on the Camino. A number of major walks from France converged at St Jean – that from Arles, from Vezelay and Paris – and Roncesvalles was the next stop and the very first village across the Spanish border.

Many Spaniards and pilgrims of other nationalities started here, so the *albergue* was almost full but he managed to find himself a bunk bed. The first thing he felt he needed was a shower. Fortunately, one of the shower booths was free and he spent a long, and very relaxing, time letting the hot water wash over his head and his body, restoring him. Slowly, his muscles started to relax and the tightness and pain he had felt, especially in his calf muscles, started to melt away. He put on a fresh set of clothes and went out for a walk round the village. As he passed the church, he saw a notice saying that there was a Pilgrims'

Mass at eight o'clock and he decided he would attend. As it was still early, he went to the one and only bar in the village serving dinner. He saw that Gina, the New Zealander he had met the day before, was there too, and he went and sat next to her. They ordered a glass of Cava, the sparkling wine produced in various regions of Spain, and chatted about their experiences of the day. Both of them had found the climb up the Pyrenees very challenging, but having completed it, both felt very satisfied with their achievement. James remarked that if they had managed that very demanding climb on Day One of the Camino, they could probably cope with anything else. After a while, Gina left, and he went into the refectory at the back of the bar for his dinner.

It was his first experience of a pilgrims' meal. Although he thought it was pretty basic, it was hearty and healthy food, homemade and satisfying. The wine that went with it was very rough, so he bought himself a glass of Rioja *tinto*, which went down very well. When dinner was over, he made his way to the church and arrived just as the Mass was starting. The church was mainly full of pilgrims, although there were a few of what seemed to be locals. The Mass was in Spanish, but some important passages of the ritual were repeated in English, French, Italian and Basque. At the end of the Mass, there was the blessing of the pilgrims. All were asked to stand in front of the altar, while the priest intoned a hymn and said the same prayer in five different languages. He also announced the place of origin of each of the pilgrims who had arrived that day, and James felt a certain pride to hear Malta being mentioned together with some twenty other countries.

He returned to the *albergue* and started to settle down for the night. The other occupants of the large room in which he was staying were also unpacking their things, changing into nightclothes or chatting together. He got into his sleeping bag and lay down on his bunk bed. He was exhausted and was soon fast asleep but awoke in the middle of the night. He became aware of just how noisy the room was. People were snoring, tossing and turning, and a great deal of sighing, coughing and other sounds contributed further to the cacophony. It must have been all these that woke him up.

Once awake, he found it hard to go back to sleep so, in his mind, he started to go over the sequence of events that had brought him here.After some two hours, he managed to fall asleep again and only woke up when his neighbours were already up, busy packing their rucksacks. He jumped out of bed and rushed to the bathroom to get himself ready. Then, after having a small breakfast, he set off. It was a beautiful morning, albeit quite chilly. The scenery was beautiful, and the walk was a lot easier than it had been the day before. He was walking mainly downhill on a gentle slope. During that day, he met and walked with a number of other pilgrims. Apart from Gina, whom he bumped into a couple of times during the day, he met several other people, including two South African men, a Canadian couple, two German ladies and a Korean student. He thought to himself how very international it was.

He pressed on towards his destination and felt that he was starting to get into his stride, although he realised that this was still the beginning and it could be quite different later on, when the strain started to take its toll. He passed through the small village of Larrasoaña, where most of the other pilgrims stopped for the night but carried on, as he had set his sights on Zuriain, some five kilometres further on. When he got there, the one and only *albergue* was full but the municipal authorities had a card up their sleeve. There was an empty school in the village, and they were using the classrooms as bedrooms for the pilgrims, so he found himself settling into a classroom, which he thought was rather quaint. He had never slept in a school before! There was only one other person sharing the room with him, so it promised to be a lot quieter than the previous night had been. However, he had to make do with a cold shower, as there were no hot water facilities.

In the village centre, he found a bar where everyone seemed to be hanging out. It was very lively, not least because two young Spaniards were playing their guitars and singing. The songs sounded wistful and rather sad and all those present listened intently and clapped after each song. When the two musicians took a break, the conversation erupted again, with everyone trying to recount his experiences of the day. James had already come to realise that the first questions one was asked on the Camino were, 'Where are you from?', 'Where did you start walking from?' and 'Where do you plan to walk to?'.

Soon after these details were dispensed with, the conversation would turn to more personal matters. He found that people really opened up and talked about very personal and intimate experiences and feelings. It was as though all the usual restraints had been removed and people went back to a child-like sense of trust and openness. He wished that he could be as open about himself, but there was one part of him that had to remain hidden and which he could not talk about.

He had felt the need to record his experiences and thoughts therefore, while in Paris, he had bought himself a Moleskine notebook and a couple of pens. He was keeping a journal with an account of his daily walk and experiences. He also wanted to record a short 'thought of the day' that would encapsulate the day's events and his own feelings. He decided to return to bring his diary up to date. Once there, he let his thoughts flow and wrote about all he had seen and felt throughout that day. Soon, a bell rang to announce that 'lights-out' was in ten minutes, so he hurriedly finished off his writing, stowed his notebook in the rucksack and climbed into his sleeping bag.

He lay in bed, too keyed up to sleep. He thought that he was starting to understand what this whole walk was about. There was a common purpose among all who walked it and, as a result of this, a great sense of camaraderie. He also thought that there were other things. One was outside one's normal surroundings and was not bound by the usual social mores, which dictated a certain reserve when meeting new people. Moreover, many may have left their cares and troubles behind, unlike him, however.

Despite the fact that the Camino had provided him with welcome distractions from his troubled thoughts, he still could not forget or put them aside for very long. They would sneak back every so often, even when he was enjoying the sights and sounds of nature or conversing with other pilgrims. However, he was starting to detect a slight change already. Before he left Malta, these thoughts had been uppermost in his mind almost all the time, and he felt a great sense of guilt and hopelessness. Although the sense of guilt was still very much present, there were now the glimmerings of a sense of hope, a hope that he might find a way to somehow expiate his crime and regain his self-respect and be able to look people in the face again.

Chapter 10

Maria had set her alarm for six o'clock, as she wanted to spend a short while in *Puente la Reina* before starting the day's walk. When it went, she groped for it desperately to switch it off before it woke everyone else in the dormitory, and then switched on her small torch to find her way to the bathroom for a shower. Soon, she was on her way out of the *albergue*. She made her way to the *Calle Mayor* and walked along it.

On the way, she stopped to admire the church of Santiago, with its 12th-century façade and portico, and a gilded statue of *Santiago Peregrino*. She had read in her guidebook about the two faces of St James – one, very warrior-like which the Spaniards called *Santiago Matamoros* (St James, the killer of Moors), and the other, *Santiago Peregrino* (St James, the pilgrim), a far gentler persona of the saint. She walked to the famous bridge that gave the town its name, the *Puente la Reina* (Queen's bridge). It had been so named to honour the name of its benefactor, Doña Mayor, the wife of King Sancho III. It was a magnificent bridge with six stone arches spanning the river Arga. Doña Mayor had ordered it built to facilitate the movement of pilgrims in medieval times.

As she left *Puente la Reina*, the heavens opened, and she

had to hastily deploy her poncho to protect herself and her rucksack. It was strange to find herself remaining mainly dry, except for her exposed legs, while walking in pouring rain. There was a certain novelty to it. At home, she would never consider walking in such conditions, and yet here, protected as she was by her poncho, it seemed quite normal and acceptable. She could see that other pilgrims had deployed their own ponchos or other waterproof gear and were walking on, regardless. After an hour or so, the rain stopped as suddenly as it had started, and it became quite warm again, so she had to remove her poncho, and then take off her rucksack to remove her jacket as well. She had needed to do this a couple of times since she started and found these changes quite tiring and costly in terms of time and effort.

After the rain stopped, it was easier to communicate with other walkers, and soon, she was deep in conversation with Silvia, a young Italian lady whom she had met a short while earlier. Silvia had started her walk from St Jean and had been walking alone for several days. She was very pleased to meet someone who could converse with her in Italian. Although Maria did not get many opportunities to practise her Italian, she slipped back into it quite easily.

She discovered that Silvia had recently separated from her husband and was walking the Camino to try to get to grips with the new realities in her life. Maria was surprised to learn that she had a son who had just turned sixteen, since she looked far too young. Silvia talked at length about her acrimonious separation and the ensuing bitter legal battle for the custody of their son. Maria tried to comfort her newfound friend, with whom she felt considerable empathy, having been through the trauma of a separation herself. Silvia was a very attractive woman in her late thirties and, while they walked together, a number of single male walkers tried to involve them in conversation, but Maria and Silvia would have none of it.

They walked on through the day. The scenery was spectacular. Vast areas of cultivation alternated with densely-forested areas, quaint, little, hilltop villages and, in the distance, a vast range of mountains. They stopped for lunch in the tiny village of Lorca and, while chatting over the meal, got to know each other a bit better. Silvia worked as a secretary to the managing director of a large Italian confectionery firm and thus, in some respects, they had similar responsibilities in their jobs.

They spoke at length about their respective lives, yet Maria stopped short of telling Silvia about what had really led to her decide to walk the Camino, since she was still reluctant to open up about her mother's accident, and her part in it. She felt quite sure that Silvia might well empathise with her, and yet she just could not bring herself to confide in anyone for the time being.

They walked on until they got to Estella, their destination for the day. It was a really vibrant town. They passed through the cobbled main street of the town and, in the centre, they came across a very wide, open flight of steps winding up the hill to the church of San Pedro, at the top. They visited this and were told by the guide in the church that it was where the kings of Navarre took their oaths of office. In her mind's eye, Maria pictured a procession of the King's court in all their finery, walking up this magnificent flight of steps to the church.

Although it was still only early afternoon, they thought that they should get to the *albergue, since* the beds would soon be taken up. Fortunately, there was space available and, after they left their rucksacks by their beds, they went for a walk round the town together. They met a few of the other pilgrims they had come across during the day and they all ended up going to dinner together in one of the restaurants along the river. It had not been a particularly strenuous day, so they both stayed as late as they could, only returning to the *albergue* just before closing time.

Chapter 11

After a restless, few hours, he managed to sleep, and this time, there were no sounds of the dormitory to disturb his sleep. He woke up feeling full of energy and all set to go. There was the usual hubbub in the nearby *albergue* as everyone got out of bed at more-or-less the same time, leading to the inevitable rush for the showers. Since he had unpacked as few items as possible, having learnt how hard it was to pack systematically in the very limited space and time one had available, he was soon ready to leave. He knew that he had a long walk ahead of him. He had set his sights on *Puente la Reina,* which was a good thirty-four kilometres away. He would be passing through Pamplona and he was sorry that he would not be spending the night there. Nevertheless, he intended to spend at least a couple of hours there on his way through it.

It was a beautiful morning, crisp and with not a cloud in the sky. He was walking alone and there were no other walkers in sight. The air was clear, and he could see the hills in the distance very distinctly while, closer at hand, were rolling fields of corn, punctuated in places by copses of tall green trees. He could feel the sounds of the countryside envelop him: the wind blowing through the trees, the sound of a distant tractor and farm hands calling to each other, the occasional bleating of sheep from one of the large flocks that he passed every so often, guided and corralled so effectively by the shepherd's dogs, the rushing of water when he crossed a small stream or walked by a river. It was balm for his soul, and he started to feel relaxed and more at peace than he had ever been in these last weeks. He made a point of not stopping to talk to any other pilgrims, as he wanted his solitary communion with nature to continue for as long as possible. While he walked, his mind alternated between a complete absence of thought, when all that passed through it were sensory perceptions, and other times when reality would intrude on his reverie and he would think deeply about his troubles, and how he could perhaps come to terms with them. It was a kind of meditation in motion and definitely superior to sitting in a chair to think. The physical movement, the changing and beautiful scenery and the sensory experiences helped to enhance it.

After some time, he saw ahead of him what he assumed was Pamplona. He crossed the river Arga and soon reached the outskirts of the city, which were modern and featureless. In a short while, the walls of the old city appeared before him and he walked through one of their gates into it. It occurred to him that, while the walls were reasonably high, they were nowhere near as impressive as the walls of Valletta. He spent some time walking around the city and visited the cathedral and its museum. Before continuing on his walk, he decided to have an early lunch, and he chose an open-air restaurant in the *Calle Mayor,* just opposite the town hall. When he had ordered his meal, various *pinchos* and a glass of white wine, he asked the waiter to tell him about what went on during the feast of San Fermin, when the running of the bulls took place. The waiter was seemingly overjoyed to be asked this as it was clearly a subject very close to his heart. He waxed lyrical about the feast, which lasted a whole week in July and about the preparations and build-up to it. The buildings and the streets would be decorated lavishly, and the main street would be lined with timber boarding to prepare for the running of the bulls. The houses along the route would be especially well decorated, with everyone competing to have the best flower boxes in their balconies. He sat there for as long as he could, watching the life in the city go by, but soon, he felt he had to proceed on to his destination. Somewhat regretfully, he left the city but promised himself that one day he would come back, preferably during fiesta time.

Soon after he left the city, ahead of him, he could see a high ridge, topped by a line of wind turbines. He knew from his guidebook that he would have to climb it, something that proved to be harder than he had thought. The final stretch reminded him a bit of his first day on the Camino when crossing the Pyrenees, but it was far shorter than that had been and he soon found himself at the top of the ridge and looking ahead towards *Puente la Reina*, which he could see in the distance. He spent a few minutes there and then started the descent down the other side of the ridge.

It was difficult and he had to proceed with a lot of caution as the path was full of loose stones and one false step would see him spraining his ankle, or worse. After some time, the path levelled off and he found himself walking along a low ridge with the ground falling away in each direction to seas of waving cornfields on either side. It was magical! Again, he was walking mainly on his own, although he could see the odd pilgrim ahead of him in the distance. After a while, he came to a point where the Camino route offered two options – he could either take a detour to the church of Eunate, or proceed directly to *Puente la Reina*. As it was mid-afternoon and he was starting to tire a bit, he decided on the shorter option.

He arrived in *Puente la Reina* and went straight to the *albergue* to reserve his bed. Thankfully, there were beds available and he got the lower unit of a double bunk in the large dormitory. After taking a shower and changing into a fresh set of clothes, he washed his used clothes and hung them out to dry in the little garden at the back. There were several pilgrims there sitting on the grass, some writing their journals, others studying their guidebooks or just chatting together.

He felt the need for company after having spent the whole day walking on his own and set his sights on a group of four women who were chatting together in what sounded like American English. He went up to talk to them and asked them where they were from. They proved to be Canadian and all four of them lived in Toronto. It was a city he had never visited, although he had heard a good bit about it. Many Maltese migrants, who had gone to live in Canada, usually ended up there. All four of the ladies were in their mid-fifties. One of them was an experienced pilgrim who had walked the Camino a couple of times before and she was clearly the leader of the group. The other three seemed to depend on her a lot.

He invited them to join him for a drink and they walked to a bar overlooking the river and the spectacular arched bridge. They sat on the terrace sipping their glasses of *cava* and watching the day wane as the sun set across the river. The women were very curious about Malta, and they asked James all sorts of questions. They had a vague notion of its location and size, but they were surprised to learn not just how small it really was but also the importance it had enjoyed because of its strategic position in the centre of the Mediterranean. He found their company very relaxing, especially the fact that he could converse with them in English, rather than having to speak Italian or trying to make himself understood to French, German or Spanish speakers, as had been the case over the last few days. They decided to go on to dinner together in one of the tapas bars they had seen in the centre and, on the way there, they had their *credencial* stamped. James had been doing this religiously every day, sometimes even twice a day, and his *credencial* was starting to fill out nicely. Some of the stamps were quite beautiful and their diversity was so interesting. The majority came from the *albergues* but some of them had been collected in churches and town halls, while some others had come from bars or restaurants.

There was a bewildering selection of tapas to choose from the range on offer. He had learnt the names of a couple of them so far, and particularly liked the *Pimientos de Padron* – grilled, small green peppers heavily seasoned with salt and pepper – and *Patatas Bravas*, potatoes in a spicy tomato sauce. They decided to order a selection, which they could share, and in that way, they could each sample as many different ones as possible. The waiter helped them to choose the more interesting ones. The ladies said that they were hoping to walk all the way to Santiago and James half-jokingly asked them how their husbands had agreed to do without their very good company for so long. They replied unanimously that they had all agreed that they needed some girlie time, while their husbands could indulge their passion for golf in peace and quiet. It worked well for both parties! As they partook of more of the very drinkable Rioja, the conversation became ever more animated, and they laughed a lot. James felt very relaxed in their company and for the first time, his troubles receded well into the background, although he was aware that they would probably come back when the effects of the wine and the good company had worn off. Suddenly, it occurred to him that it was getting close to ten when the *albergue* closed its doors, so they paid the bill and hurried back. They wished each other goodnight and hoped to meet the next day.

Chapter 12

Her dreams woke her up several times that night. Although her evening with Silvia had been a good one and she had felt quite relaxed before falling asleep, her dreams had been very disturbing. She could not recall any of them, except for odd snatches, but they left her feeling disorientated and worried. She managed to fall asleep again and awoke with everyone else. It struck her how the dormitory seemed to come alive within a very short span of time. There would be the odd pilgrim who would rise well before anyone else but, in general, everyone seemed to wake at the same time.

She looked for Silvia, who was sleeping in another part of the dormitory, and they left the *albergue* together after a quick coffee and snack. It was a beautiful morning with the sun shining and a host of pilgrims setting off for the day. All this helped Maria to get out of the feeling of disorientation that she had been experiencing and soon, she and Silvia were making good progress. Shortly after leaving Estella, they passed through the little hamlet of Irache and there, near the Benedictine monastery, they came across the *Fuente Irache,* a wine fountain where pilgrims could fortify themselves with free red wine. Traditionally, pilgrims would fill their conch shell with the free-flowing wine. Both Maria and Silvia were carrying the conch shells they had bought at the start of the Camino. These shells had become a symbol of St James, something to do with the legend of his return to Galicia in Spain after his death. Although it was still early morning, Maria and Silvia did not want to miss out on this freebie, so they held their conch shells beneath the faucet and poured themselves a generous helping of the wine.

They walked on through a forest of pine and oak. It was shady and cool beneath the trees and the ground was soft underfoot with fallen leaves and pine needles, a welcome change from walking on asphalt. After a time, they stopped at a small glade in the forest to have a snack and remove one of their layers of clothing, since the day was warming up. They sat together on the thick trunk of a large fallen tree. Silvia turned to Maria, and asked her, "How long ago did you decide to walk the Camino, Maria?"

"It was only quite recently. I heard about it from a friend who was very enthusiastic about it."

"But what was it that attracted you to it?"

"I was going through a difficult period in my life and felt the need to get away from Malta and to spend some time thinking about where I am headed."

"Well, we've both been through a separation from our husbands, and it can be very traumatic. It has taken me some time to start to get over my own separation and of course, there is still the matter of our son, a burning issue. Despite everything my ex-husband has done, I would still be ready to treat him fairly when it comes to sharing access to our son, whereas he has never stopped trying to take far more than his fair share."

"How does your son feel about it?" Maria asked.

"Well, he prefers to be with me, in general, but then there are things that he prefers to do with his father, such as playing football, camping and so on. I have tried to engage with him on this level, too, but it isn't always easy. But what about yourself, Maria? What is it that is troubling you?"

Maria was dying to confide in her new friend but she still could not bring herself to talk about the circumstances of her mother's death, so she restricted herself to giving a redacted version,

"I lost my mother some weeks ago. We were very close, and her death came only one year after I had lost my father. I feel well and truly orphaned now. I have a sister, with whom I get on very well, and she has two lovely children, whom I adore, but I miss not having a husband or, at least, a partner. Since I broke up with my husband, Tom, I have had a few relationships, but nothing really worked. I guess I am now more cautious than I would have been in the past. Once bitten, twice shy, I guess."

They felt a certain rapport towards each other because their circumstances were, in some ways, similar and they could identify with the pain and the uncertainty that each of them felt. It gave them a sense of companionship and a feeling of wanting to help each other, thereby helping themselves too.

They walked on in silence for a time, awed by the majesty of the forest they were walking through and the silence that reigned there. They could see no other pilgrims. The path meandered among the tall trees and some light filtered through the dense foliage, producing a variegated effect. Occasionally, when they passed through a clearing in the forest, they would catch a glimpse of a tall conical hill in the distance. After a while, the forest thinned out and soon they were in open countryside and, a short distance away, was the tall hill they had glimpsed before. It was the hill of Monjardin, which rose to a great height straight out of the plain and low down, on its flanks, was the little village of *Villamayor de Monjardin*. They stopped there for some lunch and to have their *credencial* stamped. The little restaurant they chose had a small and shady internal courtyard with vines growing up the side and trellised above. It was a delightful cool and shady space.

The owner welcomed them, sat them down at a table in one corner of the courtyard and launched into a detailed description of the menu and his suggested choices. They opted for a light meal since they still had some distance to walk to their final destination of the day. The trout was fresh, and they chose a salad to go with it. After a short while, other pilgrims started to arrive and soon the little courtyard had filled up and it was abuzz with animated conversation and laughter. The wine flowed quite freely in this establishment, with the owner going round and offering his customers one glass of icy cold cava after another.

A great feeling of warmth and contentment settled on the two new friends. Although they chatted, they were relaxed enough in each other's company not to feel the need to talk constantly. In one of the pauses in the conversation, Maria looked around the courtyard at the other people there. They were almost all pilgrims. She recognised a couple of people they had walked past that morning or even a day or so ago. It struck her how one met people, then lost them, then met them again. It was a bit like life, where one could be estranged, or separated, from certain friends for a time, only to then meet them and get close to them once again later. It reminded her how in this respect, as in so many others, the Camino was a bit like life in microcosm.

They stretched out their stay in the restaurant as long as they dared. The afternoon was well advanced when they eventually set off, very reluctantly. They had not wanted to leave that cool haven to face the heat and the physical effort of walking on, but they had no choice. There were still some eleven or twelve kilometres left to Los Arcos, their destination for the day. Since they left the restaurant fairly late, they did not want to take the risk of not finding a bed when they arrived, so they phoned one of the private *albergues* to book themselves a bed each. It was possible to do this with the private ones, although the municipal and the church-run *albergues* did not accept bookings, since they operated on a first come/first served basis.

 From then on, at least, the path followed a gentle descent almost all the way, so it was not too demanding physically. After a while, they got their second wind, and were able to keep up a good pace. As they rounded the little valley between two hills, they could see the town of Los Arcos and soon they had entered it. Their *albergue* was easy to find as it was on the main route through the town.

After they checked in, they noted that the accommodation was somewhat more comfortable than what they had experienced in the last two nights. They had a locker each, as well as a chair by their bunk bed, while the toilet facilities were more generous and better fitted out. Maria felt very pleased, and it suddenly struck her how she had changed in just a few days. Had she been faced with accommodation like this on any of her usual trips, she would have raised her nose at it and found it totally unacceptable, whereas in the context of the Camino, the slight improvement in the accommodation seemed like cause to celebrate.

After they had unpacked and had a shower, they went for a walk round the town. The historic centre was not very large and soon they had seen most of it. They stopped in front of the main church of Santa Maria, in the main square of the same name, and Maria noticed that a number of people were streaming into the church, so they went in to have a look. A Mass was just about to start. The organ was playing, and a small girls' choir was singing from the organ loft. Maria wanted to stay on for the Mass, but she had no idea whether Silvia was a practicing Catholic, although she suspected that she might be. So, she tactfully asked Silvia how she would feel if she were to stay on for the Mass.

"Yes, I would very much like to stay too," Silvia replied "However, I was not sure whether to suggest it to you."

"Good, then we agree. Let's stay."

The church soon filled up with both locals and other pilgrims. While they waited, Maria looked around her. It was a beautiful church. 'Very early, probably Romanesque,' she thought. The heaviness of the construction, with thick, circular columns and heavy stone arches, gave a tremendous feeling of solidity but this was offset by the more delicate additions, such as the retablo, the pulpit and the other furniture. The music was heavenly. She could not identify it, but the choir was singing in Latin rather than in Spanish, and some of the locals were joining in. Soon the Mass started.

She knew the ritual well, so she was able to follow until it came to the homily, when she only picked up the odd word here and there where they resembled Italian. She thought that the priest was delivering a very impassioned speech, but she had no idea what it was about, although she did notice that the locals appeared to be quite chastened by it all. Her mind started to wander, and she felt a glow inside her. Being in that beautiful church with that lovely music and with like-minded people gave her a great sense of contentment and peace. The physical effort she had had to make in order to get here also contributed to the feeling of contentment. Silvia, she noticed, seemed to be engrossed in the Mass too and was participating actively. It was her first Mass and Communion in some days and it affected her deeply. When the Mass was over, the two friends made their way silently out of the church, deep in thought. It was only when they walked down the length of the main square that they got out of their reverie and started to talk.

"That was quite an experience, Maria. Thank you for suggesting it. I'd missed going to Mass and I wish there were more opportunities to do so on the Camino."

"Yes, I agree. I thought everything was just perfect: the music, the choir, the Mass of course, and the church itself. I wish I could have understood what the priest was saying, though. He seemed to be getting quite hot under the collar at one stage."

"Yes, I thought so too, and the locals seemed to be quite sheepish by the time he had finished with them."

"Well, it's dinner time now. I could really do with something nice to eat. Shall we go to that little place we saw earlier? It looked quite reasonable."

"Sure".

Chapter 13

The four Canadian ladies, whom he had secretly nicknamed 'The Toronto Four', were already at breakfast when he turned up, so he joined them at their table. They were talking about their last holiday together in British Columbia. He learnt that they had been friends for a very long time, and that they had continued to meet even after their marriages. As a result, the husbands had become good friends too, and having found a common interest in golf, they had no objection when their wives decided to go off on their own for a long weekend to Georgian Bay or Quebec City. All four of them lived close to the Toronto Beaches and they told him that would meet most mornings, when the weather was kind, for an early morning walk along the famous boardwalk facing Lake Ontario.

They started off together, but he found that he had to slow his pace down somewhat for them to keep up with him, which suited him fine as he liked to walk a bit more slowly to savour the early mornings and enjoy the silence. His companions must have felt the same way because they spoke little and the five of them walked together in silence for a couple of hours, until they got to the little village of Lorca. They decided to stop there for a mid-morning snack at what seemed like a very popular watering hole. There were many pilgrims there having an early lunch or a late breakfast. A number had taken off their boots to give their feet some respite and the smell of damp and sweaty socks pervaded the atmosphere. They ordered the usual *boc-cadillo con jamon,* a large baguette stuffed with ham, and an orange juice or a coffee. He asked them whether they came to Europe often.

"Not as often as we would like to", said Kathy, their de facto leader. "We tend to travel a good bit in North America. There are some great places in Canada and the US and, scenically, they can be quite spectacular, like the National Parks and so on. Yet there is so much history and culture in Europe that we do not have. In our country, anything that dates over a hundred years is considered old but here you are talking of a history spanning hundreds or even thousands of years. On top of that, the sheer cultural diversity that you encounter in Europe is something we certainly do not have."

"So, what decided you all to come and walk the Camino now?" James asked.

Sheila pipped in and said, "Well, Kathy has been telling us about it for so long, we just felt we had to try it," adding, "and we wanted to see how good she would be at leading us through it."

"She's actually done pretty well so far, although at times I feel that she walked us off our feet!" added Julia, with a wide grin.

While they ate their sandwiches, the conversation turned to more serious matters. Three of the four ladies had had brushes with cancer, in one form or another. They had all been treated successfully and returned regularly to their doctors for checkups, but they all wondered nonetheless whether their illness would return at any time. James was surprised at how matter-of-fact they were about it. They did not seem to be overly worried and they seemed to be quite philosophical about it all. He admired them for that, and he wondered how he would feel if he had something like that hanging over his head. That thought reminded him that, in fact, he did have something hanging over his head, something that, in a way, was even worse than that faced by the four ladies, because it was something for which he had been responsible, rather than something fortuitous. In the last few days, it had been less on his mind than before, due largely to the change of scene and the fact that he was so taken up with walking, although there had been many moments, especially in the early mornings, while he was walking alone, that it had come back to haunt him. His companions must have noticed that his mind had wandered off.

"Are you all right, James?" asked Kathy. "You seem to be quite distracted. Has our conversation upset you?"

"I am sorry, ladies. I was thinking back to something that the conversation reminded me of."

At that, they did not probe any further and they went on to talk about other things. It was time to move on too. James had set his sights on walking to Monjardin that day and he told his friends that. They did not think they could get that far and they said they would stop in Estella instead. When they got there, he accompanied them to the *albergue* where they were planning to stay, and they exchanged contact information.

"Well, ladies, it's been great walking with you. I do hope that we shall meet again on the Camino and if not, perhaps one day in Canada … or maybe Malta."

They said their goodbyes and he walked on out of the town and started on the long trek to Monjardin. As he passed by the *Fuente de Irache*, he saw a number of his fellow walkers stopping to fill their shells with the free wine, but he carried on walking. The last thing he needed now was red wine. It would make him drowsy and render the remaining kilometres more of a challenge. Soon, he found himself walking through a majestic forest all on his own. The tall pine trees stretched up towards the sky, and as the familiar sounds of the countryside died away, there was a great stillness, where the only sounds were those of his boots tramping on the pine needles.

He thought back to his all too brief encounter with the Canadian ladies and he hoped that he would bump into them again, although he doubted it would happen. He was planning to cover rather more ground than they were and thus they might never meet again. He was saddened by this and felt a certain sense of loss. Then he thought about the loss the old lady's family had sustained and that made him feel worse still. 'What,' he asked himself, 'had he achieved so far, in terms of coming to terms with his problem and of atoning for it?' Yes, it was true that the walk entailed some considerable discomfort, and even suffering, at times, but he felt that this was a long way off from what he felt he needed. However, there were some small glimmerings of hope to be found in the effect the walk was having on him.

As he walked out of the forest, he caught sight of the very tall, conical hill with the village of *Villamayor de Monjardin* on its flank, his destination for the day. He made straight for the *albergue,* as he was dying to shower and change into fresh clothes. He also needed to call home to see how Peter was getting on with managing things at the office. He felt quite refreshed after his shower and a brief rest, and so he went out for a short walk round the village. There were very few people around and he stopped for a beer in one of the bars along the main street. He was the only person there and he started chatting with the barman who complained that, since few of the guidebooks placed Monjardin at the end of a leg, or stage, of the Camino, very few pilgrims actually spent the night there. Although quite a few did stop for lunch, this still meant a lot less income for the village.

He went on to say that things had been difficult in Spain with unemployment, especially among young people. Many of them were moving to the large cities like Madrid and Barcelona to try and find work and, as a result, small villages like Monjardin were losing many of their young people and becoming geriatric villages. He railed against the government for what he saw as its failure to address the country's problems. James was enjoying his company and decided to take whatever the bar could offer by way of food, rather than moving away to seek a proper restaurant. The barman managed to rustle up some quite decent tapas including James's favourite *Pimientos de Padron*. He told his new friend that he planned to walk as far as Logroño the following day. The barman seemed sceptical, and said, "*Señor*, it is nearly forty kilometres up to Logroño. Why do you not stop in *Torres del Rio* or perhaps Viana? That would be much easier."

"Yes, perhaps I will, but I had really been hoping to spend tomorrow night in Logroño that, I am told, is an interesting city."

"That it is! The cathedral is very beautiful, and it has a very unusual façade. The *Plaza Mayor* has lots of nice outdoor restaurants, and it is always full of people."

On that note, James said goodnight to the barman and made his way back to the *albergue*. The few pilgrims who were staying there were already fast asleep, so he crept quietly into the dormitory and changed into his night things as quietly as he could, switched off his torch, and went straight to sleep.

Chapter 14

Maria woke up to the sound of bells ringing. The *albergue* was quite close to the parish church of Santa Maria and the bells started ringing early in the morning just before the first Mass at six o'clock. She saw other pilgrims starting to stir, so she decided to get out of bed and get herself ready for the day. There was a long trek to Logroño, so she wanted to make an early start. The bathroom was still deserted, and she was able to get a long, relaxing shower. After she had dressed and packed her rucksack, she went to look for Silvia, who was in another part of the dormitory and found her without difficulty. Silvia was struggling out of bed, looking quite wan. Maria asked her whether she was feeling all right.

"No, I'm not. I had a bad night. I slept very little and was feeling quite sick most of the time," replied Silvia.

"What is the matter? Is it your stomach or bowels?"

"Yes. Definitely. I must have eaten something that didn't agree with me."

"But we ate the same things last night, Silvia."

"Yes, we did but, if you remember, at the end of the meal I ordered a caramel pudding while you did not. It must have been off. Look, I think I need to lie low for a bit and try to catch up on the sleep I lost last night, but I don't want to hold you up. You must carry on."

"I really could stay with you, if you wish," Maria offered, anxiously.

"No, I think you should carry on. In a few hours I'll be well, and I'll try and catch up with you. If not today, I will certainly manage to do so by tomorrow."

"All right," said Maria, "but call me if anything changes."

Maria set off on the day's walking, immediately finding herself faced by a steep climb shortly after she left the town. She felt sorry that Silvia was unwell and hoped that she would recover quickly, and they could meet again. She had really enjoyed her new friend and was going to miss her companionship. Later in the day, she would call to see how she was faring. Soon she reached *Torres del Rio* and decided to stop there for a mid-morning snack. While she waited for her *bocadillo* to be brought to her, she watched as a steady stream of pilgrims walked by. Some stopped at the same bar, while others carried on walking.

She exchanged a few words with a group of German pilgrims at the next table, but did not stay too long, and started walking again as soon as she had finished eating. There was still a long way to go to her destination. She spent the whole day walking on her own, as she did not feel like talking to anyone, maybe due to Silvia's unexpected illness or perhaps her own thoughts coming to the surface. The day passed like a dream. She walked through Viana without even stopping for lunch, and it was only as she approached Logroño that she came back to her senses. She passed a sign that read that she was entering the province of *La Rioja*, one of the smallest of Spain's provinces that was famous for its wine. From this border, she could already see the city of Logroño close by. She soon reached the centre and found the *albergue*. When she got there, she took one look at it and decided, that on this day, she was going to treat herself to a little break from the normal routine. She needed to get her clothes washed and dried properly and a good night's sleep in a quiet and comfortable place, so she started to look for a hotel. Finally, she opted for the *Marques de Vallejo*, which was very close to the main square. It was a small, but very attractive hotel. Maria asked for a room and was told, much to her relief, that there was a single room with bathroom available. She went up, spent a half hour lying in and enjoying the unbelievable luxury of a hot bath. She then dressed and went to look for a laundry. The hotel receptionist recommended one that was quite close. Later, she went on to explore the city centre.

The cathedral was most unusual. It had a very plain exterior except for the very large and ornate doorway. The interior was in Gothic style, with cross-vaulted roofing and with Renaissance additions. She stopped to say a little prayer for her mother, for herself and for Silvia to recover quickly. When she walked out of the cathedral, the streets were beginning to fill up with the citizens who had just finished work and were enjoying a stroll up and down the main streets or seating themselves at the many outdoor cafes and bars scattered around the square.

She suddenly remembered that the hotel had offered her a free cocktail after six p.m. She looked at her watch and saw that it was nearly time, so she walked back to the hotel. There were three couples in the bar sipping at their complimentary drinks. None of them seemed in the least bit approachable and she thought to herself, 'How very different this was to what happened on the Camino, where everyone was so ready to communicate with everybody else.' So, adopting a rather reproving air, she also took her drink on her own. After collecting her clothes from the laundry, she went on to the main square to have her dinner. She had spotted a nice-looking restaurant right opposite the cathedral and had booked a table. After ordering a glass of cava, she chose her meal. She was starting to understand the menu and she selected *croquetas* and *pimientos de padron,* followed by pork. She had decided to really spoil herself that evening, and also ordered a platter of the local cheeses and a glass of Rioja. By the end of it, she was feeling very satisfied and relaxed. She called Silvia to see how she was getting on and was relieved to hear that Silvia had made a complete recovery after some hours of rest. In fact, she was on the road again, although she would certainly stop short of Logroño.

She then called Johanna. It had been some days since they had spoken and her sister had been quite anxious, so she was very pleased to hear Maria's voice. She asked Maria how she was getting on. Maria told her all about her experiences and how she was feeling about it all. Johanna was quite relieved to hear things seemed to be going well. Then, Maria asked her whether there had been any developments regarding the accident, and whether the police had any leads on the driver of the car. Johanna replied that, regretfully, there was nothing new. The police seemed to have drawn a complete blank.

Once her calls were over, she sat on in the restaurant, watching life go by in the square. Things were in full swing. All the outdoor tables of the various restaurants and bars lining the square were full and many locals were still walking up and down the streets, occasionally stopping to chat with family and friends. There was a general hubbub of conversation. Everyone seemed to be having a good time. Suddenly, a group of some ten young men, dressed in traditional and very colourful costumes, and armed with guitars and mandolins, came into the square, took up a position in front of the cathedral and started to play music and sing. Maria recognised some of the songs and their playing sounded wonderful. She asked one of the waiters what it was all about.

"It is *La Tuna, señora*," he replied.

"What is that? I don't understand."

"They are university students, who dress up in traditional dress and sing old songs and *serenatas* to earn some money. It is a tradition that goes back many hundreds of years."

She noticed that after every three or four songs, one of them would go round collecting money from the spectators. All the people walking up and down the square had stopped to watch, as had those seated in the outdoor restaurants, like Maria. It was truly magical, and she was mesmerized by their skill, finding the music and the singing so exciting. They played for a good hour, and she enjoyed every minute of it. It was a fitting end to the day and, after they had finished their performance and left, she made her way back to the hotel. She had another long day coming up and it was already quite late.

Chapter 15

It was still dark when he started off. He had risen very early as he was determined to get to Logroño. There were no other walkers around and very few sounds too. It was still too early for the birds to start their song and none of the farmers were in their fields yet. It gave him, as it always did, some satisfaction to be up so early and to feel that he had a lead on the world. Little by little, the world around him came alive. Dawn was followed by a beautiful sunrise and soon he was seeing signs of life.

As he passed through *Los Arcos*, he noticed that everything was still shut. 'The Spaniards did not believe in making an early start in the mornings,' he thought. Soon, he was out in the countryside again, heading towards *Torres del Rio*. He stopped there for brunch and the bar he chose was clearly a popular one, as there were no free tables. He went up to a young lady sitting on her own and asked her whether he could sit at her table as there were no other free places. She replied in perfect English, and he realised that she was British, and probably from the London area, judging by her accent. He thanked her and sat down.

"This seems to be a really popular place," he said.

"It certainly is but that's not too surprising, because it's an obvious stopping-off place for late breakfast or early lunch for anyone heading to Logoño," she replied.

"Is that where you are heading to?"

"I'm still not sure. I may stop off in Viana as I was told it's an interesting little town and they have a great *albergue*, you know, one of those with lots of atmosphere. It's run by an order of monks and the *albergue* is, in fact, part of the old monastery, and is very atmospheric, I am told."

"That sounds great. I have heard about places like that, but I haven't managed to stay at any yet. As for me, I am trying to get to Logroño tonight."

"Wow! That's quite a way. I try to limit my walking to twenty-five k max per day."

"Where did you start your Camino from?" he asked.

"From Pamplona. I couldn't face the huge climb over the mountains before that. I spent a couple of days there before starting off. It was my very first introduction to Spain, and Pamplona is a very special city. I love Hemingway and he wrote so much about it."

"Unfortunately, I only passed through it, and saw very little of the city, but I shall return one day. By the way, my name is James … and yours is?"

"I'm Lisa and I live in Kingston. That's a part of London, you know."

"Yes. I have been quite close to it. I stayed in Richmond once. I love London and I feel so much at home there."

"Where are you from, then? You speak English very well, but you are not English. I have been trying to place you and my best bet, at the moment, is Greek or Italian, although I don't think either is quite right."

"Neither of the two, I'm afraid. I'm Maltese."

"Ah, that's it! Of course!" she said, as she slapped the table. "I've met some people from Malta in London, and I should have recognised the accent. Funnily enough, I met a Maltese pilgrim yesterday in Los Arcos, which is where I started from this morning."

"Really! That's amazing because we are such a small country and I imagined that very few Maltese would be walking the Camino."

"Well, the person I met was a young lady. Very nice person! I didn't get to ask her name but she said that she was hoping to walk all the way to Santiago so we might well bump into each other again."

"You never know. I have noticed how one meets people along the way, then loses them and sometimes meets them again … or not."

He wondered who this Maltese woman could possibly be. Who knows, it could be someone he knew, and this would not be unusual, given Malta's small population and the very active social life in the country. He looked at his watch and realised that it was getting on and it was time for him to leave. He said goodbye to Lisa and said he hoped they would meet again. He walked uninterruptedly after that, reaching Logroño at dusk. He made his way straight to the *albergue*, hoping he would be able to get a bed at this late hour. At first, the pretty *hospitalera* behind the counter told him that they were full but, when she saw his crestfallen look, she said that perhaps they could somehow put him up if he didn't mind sleeping outdoors in a covered terrace. They had a bed available in one of the loggias at the back of the *albergue*, overlooking the garden. He accepted readily and the *hospitalera* showed him to his bed. He was inclined to lie down and go to sleep straight away after his long walk, but then thought to himself that he must, at least, have a look at the cathedral he had heard so much about. Perhaps afterwards, if he could summon up enough energy, he could also take a nightcap in the main square.

When he got there, he found that the cathedral was closed but he was at least able to admire its unusual exterior. Then he found himself a table in one of the bars in the square. He ordered a glass of *Rioja Reserva* and looked around the square. It was full of people having their dinner or just drinking. They seemed to be mainly locals, although he could see a few young and middle-aged people who were clearly pilgrims. He wondered whether the Maltese woman that Lisa had mentioned meeting in *Los Arcos* was anywhere around. Soon, his tiredness caught up with him again, and he decided to turn in. As he was leaving the square, he saw a group of young people in fancy costumes who set themselves up at one end of the square and started to play their instruments and accompanying the music with their singing. He asked one of the passers-by what it was all about.

"They are called *La Tuna*. They are university students who play and sing to raise money for themselves so they can continue with their studies. It is a very old tradition."

He was tempted to stay and watch, but his tiredness got the better of him and, somewhat regretfully, he made his way back to the *albergue* and to his bed.

Chapter 16

Maria made the most of her stay in the hotel. She still woke up very early, but stayed on in bed for a while longer, enjoying the softness of the mattress and the wonderful down pillows. She then treated herself to a long and blissful shower and, after she had dressed, she went down to breakfast. It was a buffet style breakfast and a very good one, too. She helped herself to some *Jamon Iberico*, the wonderful ham of Spain from the region of Extremadura, *croquetas* and a slice of the famous Spanish *tortilla,* an omelette with potatoes included in the mix. She did not want to overeat, even though the large range of tasty items on offer tempted her.

When she had finished and had her first coffee of the day, she paid her bill, asked the receptionist to stamp her *credencial* and got on her way. The route followed by the Camino pleasantly surprised her. It consisted of a landscaped park stretching from the centre to the outer perimeter of the city. It was most attractive and put her into a good mood and all set to face the day.

Some six kilometres after leaving the city, she saw that she was approaching what appeared to be a small lake. When she arrived, there was a sign announcing that this was the *Pantano de la Grajera.* Beneath this name, there was an explanation in several languages, including English, which said that this was a man-made water reservoir for the city of Logroño and for the region around it. The Camino followed the edge of the lake and very soon, she found herself in a small rest area with benches. There were a few pilgrims sitting down and taking photos and she stopped to take in the beautiful view and to have a short rest.

James arose quite early and, when he got to the refectory to have breakfast, he looked out for Lisa, in case she had finally made it to Logroño, but she was not there. He collected the stamp on his *credencial* and set off. It was a beautiful day with not a cloud in the sky. He had had a good night, free of bad dreams or periods of wakefulness, and was looking forward to the day's walk, which would be a good bit shorter than that of the previous day. The walk was very pleasant indeed, as the planners of the city had created a park through which the Camino ran all the way out of the city, rather than passing through featureless suburbs or, worse still, through some industrial area. When he reached the open countryside, he again started to savour its sights, sounds and smells, which raised his spirits so much. He was starting to feel a bit less oppressed by his guilt.

He walked on and soon noticed that he was approaching a small lake. As he got closer, he saw the beautiful scene it presented. In the distance, was a range of snow-capped mountains, while in the middle distance there were endless fields of corn and, close by, was the lake with its clear blue waters and its margins lined with trees. He thought he would stop and take some photographs and sought a good spot from where to take them.

Soon, he came across a small rest area with a few benches with an unobstructed view of the whole panorama. He took shot after shot, and then rested for a few minutes on one of the benches, where he ate a snack he had brought along with him. While he ate, he looked around him. There were some other pilgrims there, two young men, an elderly couple and a young lady on her own. He wanted to get a photo of himself in that location, with that wonderful scene in the background. He could have taken a selfie, but he did not have a selfie stick so he looked around to see if he could ask one of the people there to take it for him. The two young men looked like they were about to leave, and the elderly couple were too engrossed in each other, so he went up to the young lady and asked her whether she could take his photo with the lake in the background.

"Yes, of course!" she replied.

James stood with his back to the lake facing her from a couple of metres away. He immediately sensed her perfume. It was quite subtle but noticeable and it reminded him of something or someone. She was wearing dark-blue hiking trousers and a white tee shirt. Round her neck, she had a checked scarf or bandana and no headgear. She had a great figure and was quite tall, almost his own height. He found her very attractive.

"Could you move slightly to the left, please?" she said. "I'd like to get those mountains in the background well into the picture."

He did as she instructed and waited while she moved sideways and forwards to try and get the best angle. She must have taken several shots. When she had finished, she looked at the results of her work, nodded and handed his phone back to him and said with a smile: "There's a couple of good shots there. It's a great place for a photo. Say, would you take one or two of me, please?"

"With pleasure," he replied, and again the two of them re-enacted the slow dance of getting into position and finding the best angle. He handed her phone back to her and as she looked at them, he asked, "Are they OK?"

"They're great, and thanks for taking them. You must be Maltese. I would recognise the accent anywhere."

"Yes, I am," he replied. "Tell me, were you in Los Arcos the night before last?"

"Yes, I was. What made you think so?"

"Well, yesterday, while walking to Logroño, I met this girl from London who told me that she had met a Maltese lady in Los Arcos and, I'm thinking that there can't be very many Maltese ladies walking the Camino at this moment in time. In fact, yesterday evening I went to have a late drink in the square at Logroño, and I was wondering whether any of the women I saw there were the one from Malta that Lisa, the London girl, had mentioned."

"What time was that?" she asked.

"It must have been around nine thirty or ten. Just as I was leaving, a group of Spanish youngsters were playing and singing in the square. They sounded great and I would have loved to stay and watch them, but I was too tired."

"How amazing. I was there at the same time, but I watched them right through to the very end. They were very good indeed. Someone I asked told me they are called *La Tuna,* university students who play and sing to raise money to cover their studies and books."

"Yes, that's right. I was told the same thing too before I left."

"Where are you planning to walk to today?" he asked her.

"Well, I would like to get as far as Azofra, if I can make it, otherwise I will stop a bit before, at Najera."

"I had pretty much the same thought," he said, not completely truthfully. He had already decided that he wanted to walk the further distance but having met this lady, he wanted to keep his options open. "By the way, I'm James, James Borg."

"And I am Maria Mallen."

"Is that an English name?"

"Yes. I was married to an Englishman. We separated and divorced some years ago, but I kept my married name."

"Would you mind if we walked together for a bit?" he asked somewhat tentatively.

"Sure. I would like that, except that I hope I will not slow you down. I am a fairly fast walker but maybe not as fast as you. I saw you as you were approaching, and you are pretty fast."

"Well, let's see."

And with that, they set off together. They chatted a good bit as they walked but there were periods of silence as well. They were not awkward ones, as happened with some people, but they seemed like a part of the conversation, almost like the pauses in music. They spoke about how they had come to be walking the Camino, although they both held back from divulging the real reasons for their being there. They both mentioned their intention to walk all the way, if they possibly could, and compared notes about how they planned to do that. They walked right through Navarete but, when they got to Ventosa, they were both feeling peckish.

"Maria, we should stop for lunch here in Ventosa. It looks like a nice little village and there's nothing beyond it until Najera."

"OK, let's do that, James. I'm pretty hungry and I could really do with something to eat."

They found a little bar that served food and sat at an outdoor table. It was a lovely day and not too hot, so they did not mind sitting out in the sun. All the other tables were full of pilgrims, a few of whom were chatting excitedly, while others rested, or were writing in their diaries. The bar offered a stamp for its customers, so they added one more to their collection on their *credenciales*. There was only a pilgrims' menu on offer, but it sounded good, with a soup for starters, hake as a main course and the familiar caramel pudding that the Spaniards, rather strangely, called a flan. They allowed themselves one glass of white Albariño wine, as they still had some walking to do after their lunch.

While they waited for their food to arrive, Maria found herself telling James all about why her marriage with Tom Mallen had failed and about her life as a divorcée. She told him about the various short, and generally unsatisfactory, relationships she had had since the divorce. She realised he was a good listener and it felt good to unburden herself. While she spoke, he watched her intently. There was something he found extremely attractive about her. She was definitely pretty, even beautiful, but there was more to it than just that.

There was something about her that suggested to him that this was a person one could really trust, and who would be caring and loving. He also found himself being very strongly attracted to her physically and he was very aware of her proximity at the small table where they were seated, the closeness of her legs beneath the table, and her arms resting on the tabletop. When he reached out for his glass and his hand accidentally brushed against her arm, he felt a thrill that he had not experienced in a long time.

He was deep in these thoughts when he suddenly became aware that she had stopped talking and she was looking at him questioningly. He felt himself blush slightly and said to her,

"Forgive me, I was distracted for a bit, but I was listening to all you were saying. I can imagine how difficult it must have been for you. I have never been married myself, so maybe I cannot fully comprehend what it must have been like for you, but I have had some relationships and one or two of them seemed to matter at the time so when they came to end, it felt hard too. It's actually one of the regrets I have that I never met anyone that I really wanted to marry. Most of my friends have been married and settled for some time now and have children who are growing up. I feel I have missed out on all that."

"Well, it's never too late," Maria said. "You may still meet someone with whom you will really fall in love. Although I had a traumatic marriage, I have not, by any means, given up hoping that I may yet meet the right person for me."

"Let's drink to that then," James said. "That we may both meet the right person!" They clinked their glasses and looked each other in the eyes as they raised them to their lips.

Chapter 17

That day, the rest of the walk seemed to fly by. They had adjusted their pace to each other so neither of the two felt they were having to walk too slowly or too fast. For most of the way, they spoke about themselves, their aspirations, their work, and their friends, but steered clear of the traumas that had brought them there. He would never want to tell this attractive and lovely woman what he had done. Although she was tempted to tell him what was really troubling her, she didn't feel quite ready for it yet. It was still too raw and, besides, she hardly knew him.

When they got to Najera, she must have sensed that he was ready to continue walking, so she herself suggested that they walk on to Azofra. He was pleased that she had done so, although he would have stayed on in Najera had she wanted to stop there for the night. The walk was very picturesque, as it passed through a large area of parkland with big grassy meadows and forests, and with a high range of hills in the distance. The Camino was a narrow track on soft, grassy ground, ideal to walk on. They both felt very comfortable in each other's company.

When they finally reached Azofra, they were both tired. They found the *albergue* without difficulty and managed to get the last two beds available.

"Shall we go and grab something to eat? I'm suddenly quite hungry again," James suggested.

"Yes, so am I."

"Great, then let's go. I saw a place on the way into the village that looked quite nice."

They walked back to the restaurant James had seen, and Maria had to admit that she approved of his choice. It had a quaint exterior with a multitude of conch shells decorating every square centimetre of its walls. Once they walked inside, the waiter led them to a large courtyard with a couple of olive trees, and vines growing through the overhead trelliswork. There were a number of diners already, and each table had a candle burning brightly set on it, creating a really welcoming atmosphere. They sat opposite each other in a corner of the courtyard, at another small, intimate table, as James noted. After studying the menu long and hard and discussing it together, they chose their meal. They had decided to share everything so they could get to sample many more different dishes in that way. While they waited for their food to come, James said to her,

"What made you decide to walk the Camino, Maria?

He knew that if she were to throw the question back at him, he would not be able to give her his real reason, but he sometimes liked to live dangerously.

"I guess it was partly the loss of both my parents within a short space of time but especially the fact that I feel I am quite directionless at the moment. I wanted to spend some time thinking about where I am now, where I am going and where I should be. Like you, I too would like to have a family, a husband, children and a stable home. All of that!" she replied, with a final flourish of her hand.

"And do you think that the experience has been helpful so far?"

"In some ways, yes. I find I can think better when I am walking, especially in the countryside, where it is quiet and one is surrounded by nature rather than by the din of the city, which definitely doesn't allow you to think at all. I also find that there is an aura of spirituality about it that gives me a sense of peace."

"Are you spiritual, Maria?"

"Yes, I believe I am, but not only in the religious sense. More importantly, I am spiritual in the belief that man has something special, something distinguishing us from the rest of creation, something which makes us capable of rising to great heights, but also of descending to great depths of depravity and evil. It is as though this gift we have allows us to be as good as saints, and as bad as the worst sinners. The Faith has always been an important part of my life and it also partly explains why I am here walking this Camino. What about you, James, why are you here?"

"I too have been going through a hard time. I spent years building up my firm and I gave it my all, with the result that I have neglected some aspects of my life which, I realise now, are as important, or even more important than my work. I feel I need to go through a process to work out what I need to do now to put my life back on the rails," he replied. Then he went on to add, somewhat riskily, "I also feel the need to atone for some mistakes I have made along the way."

"Well, it seems that we are both on a mission of sorts. Let's hope that we both manage to find what we are looking for."

Their meal had arrived, and they talked about lighter matters while they ate. Maria was aware of the fact that she had not enjoyed herself so much with a male companion in a long time. James was a good and sympathetic listener and was intelligent. He also seemed to be kind and honest. She found him attractive, especially when she compared him mentally with her most recent boyfriends. He certainly was a chalk above her latest, John, and way above all of the others. She was pleased with their chance meeting, and hoped that they might continue to walk together, getting to know each other better along the way.

Maria wondered how Silvia was getting on and whether she was likely to catch up with them or not. She had enjoyed her company as well and thought it would be nice if Silvia were to join them but, at the same time, she wondered whether this would hinder her from getting to know James better. She thought back to her conversation the day before with Johanna, and the disappointing lack of progress on the investigation into the accident. She still hoped that the police would catch the culprit, who would then have to pay his or her dues. However, she was now feeling slightly less vengeful than she had before she had left from Malta. It was clear to her that she was starting to dissociate herself from Malta and her normal life back home.

"A penny for your thoughts," James interrupted her reverie.

"Well, I was thinking about my sister back home," she lied. "I am very close to her and to her two children."

"Do you miss them?"

"I do, yes, and yet I was thinking to myself that I seem to be dissociating myself from my life in Malta. The Camino really seems to take one over."

"That it does!" said James, thinking that he was experiencing the same sensation, and, at times, was able to put aside the thoughts that had tormented him in Malta. The feelings of guilt and regret were still very much there, but were now diluted by the understanding that, somehow, he had to come to terms with what he had done, and go on living in the best way possible, hoping to find some way of atoning for what he had done. But how? He had decided to walk this Camino in the hope of finding some form of atonement. He wondered whether this was, in fact, happening. Were there other things he could do to assuage the guilt and remorse that he felt?

The other diners started to leave, as it was getting late and, before they knew it, James and Maria were almost alone in there. They ordered a last glass of wine and sipped it slowly. They talked little at that point, both enjoying the warm glow that they felt. While part of it was due to the food and the wine, it was mainly the mutual effect of their company. After a while, they became very conscious of the waiters' obvious impatience to get home to sleep, so they shared the bill, tipping the staff generously, and made their way back to the *albergue*.

They had been allocated top bunks in adjoining rows, so from their perch up high, they were able to see each other across a metre or less. When they had prepared themselves for bed and snuggled down, they lay there looking at each other across the narrow aisle. At first, both felt a bit self-conscious but neither of them could, or wanted, to turn away. After a short while, exhaustion overcame them, and they fell asleep.

Chapter 18

James woke up before her but stayed in bed watching her and waiting until she too opened her eyes. He saw the soft curl of hair on her forehead while, from where he was looking, her eyes seemed to be only half-closed. He could even hear her gentle breathing, and see her chest rise and fall gently with each breath. He took in her arms, which were bare as her nightdress had short sleeves. They had acquired quite a tan, since she wore short-sleeved shirts for most of the time she was walking. As more pilgrims started to rise and the noise level increased, she slowly stirred and opened her eyes. For a few instants, she had a wondering look, since she must have been dreaming, and was still crossing the threshold between sleep and wakefulness. Then her eyes focused on James, and she smiled,

"Good morning, James."

"Good morning, Maria. Did you sleep well?"

"I really did. I never stirred for one moment. I don't usually sleep so well."

"I did too," James said. "Are you ready to face the day?"

"Oh yes!"

They were soon all organised and, after collecting their stamp from the *hospitalero* at reception, they left the *albergue*.

Before they started walking, they tried to plan their walk for the day. They were not sure how far they would go, so they decided to play it by ear, and left the village. It was a beautiful morning, crisp but not too cold. The countryside was so heart-wrenchingly beautiful that it brought a lump to Maria's throat. She could see the path they were to follow stretch far into the distance below the hill they were on, as it meandered through the magical countryside. It gave them such an urge to walk and just surrender themselves to the force of gravity, which was taking them rapidly down the hill. They spoke little but felt comfortable in each other's company.

They made good time and reached the town of *Santo Domingo de la Calzada* in the late morning. Both had read that the namesake of this ancient town was a saint who, in the eleventh century, had dedicated his life to improving the Camino route for pilgrims. By this time, they had built up an appetite, so they found a restaurant in the historic centre and sat down to a meal. The waiter was insistent that they try the *cordero asado,* or roast lamb, and they did not regret taking his advice. When the steaming dish was brought to the table, the aroma was to die for. The meat was very tender and practically fell off the bone and onto the fork.

As they ate, they heard a band playing not so far away, and people cheering. They asked the waiter what was happening. He told them that the feast of Santo Domingo was on the following Sunday, but the celebrations had already started. When they finished the meal, they asked the waiter whether they could leave their rucksacks at the restaurant while they explored the town. They also told him that they were still undecided about how far to walk. He suggested that they walked as far as *Viloria de la Rioja,* where a friend of his owned a small, family-run hotel that, he claimed, was wonderful. They promptly agreed.

When they walked out of the restaurant, it seemed like all the inhabitants of the town were out on the streets partying. They made their way to the *Plaza Mayor*, where the sound of loud music was coming from a big brass band playing on a stage. The whole square was filled with people, mainly children and young people but also a few grandmothers, watching over their grandchildren like mother hens. They were all wearing the same red scarf round their necks over a white shirt, some sort of festive dress, and everyone was clearly having a great time. They made their way to the cathedral, and what a revelation it was! It was a beautiful building with an aura of serenity about the space, which affected Maria immediately. On an impulse, she knelt in one of the pews and said a small prayer. James watched and then he sat next to her until she had finished. They sat there for some minutes taking in the beauty and the atmosphere of the space until Maria rose and said that they should be on their way.

As they walked past the altar, they noticed a coop at the rear of the church containing two live fowl of some kind. They stopped to ask one of the wardens what they were, and he told them that they were there to commemorate a legendary miracle that had taken place long ago. When they pressed him to tell them more, he told them the story –

Three German pilgrims – a father, a mother and their son – had come to *Santo Domingo de la Calzada* on their way to Santiago and stayed at one of the inns. The innkeeper's daughter took a fancy to the young man, but he spurned her advances. Enraged by his refusal, she hid a silver goblet in his bed and then reported that it had been stolen. It was not long before the goblet was found under the young man's bedclothes and he was tried for theft, convicted and hanged the next day. The parents, saddened by his death, left the village, and continued their pilgrimage to Santiago. On their way back home, they passed through the village again. Their son was still hanging but, thanks to the miraculous intervention of Santo Domingo, he was alive. They rushed to the mayor's house to tell him what they had just seen and to ask him to take their son down and restore him to them.

When the parents arrived at his home, the mayor had just sat down to lunch. When they told him of the miracle, he remarked skeptically: 'That boy is as alive as these roast fowl I am about to eat!' whereupon the fowl came alive and flew away. The miracle was not lost on the flabbergasted mayor who immediately gave orders for the boy to be taken down and handed back to his parents. From that day on, there have always been two fowl in a coop at the back of the church.

As they left the cathedral, James turned to Maria, and asked, "What did you think of that story? Does anyone really believe that?"

"I'm sure they don't but I suppose it must be one of the more endearing legends along the Camino."

They went to collect their rucksacks and the waiter informed them that, in the meantime, he had called up his friend at Viloria and informed her that two pilgrims were planning to stay the night. At this point, he said rather sheepishly, "My friend asked me whether you would be wanting one room or two, and I wasn't sure what to reply."

Maria and James looked at each other briefly and gave a

nervous chuckle, until Maria swiftly informed the waiter that they would be needing two rooms.

The walk to their destination proved to be much harder than they had imagined. It was a good fifteen kilometres, and after a filling meal and a bit of wine, it proved to be even more of a challenge. When they finally reached Viloria, they found the hotel the waiter had booked for them straight away. It was called *La Posada* (The Inn). The owner met them as they entered, and she told them to follow her so that she could show them their rooms. First, she took Maria to hers, and then James to his. They were both very large rooms with a sitting area and a wonderful bathroom that included a Jacuzzi. After the rigours of the *albergues*, this was a welcome relief.

A short while later, after they had unpacked and showered, they met in the conservatory at the back of the hotel, which overlooked the very well-tended garden. Their host was there, waiting for them. She served them some tapas and asked them what they wanted to drink. She spoke English very well indeed and with hardly any accent at all. She was very pleasant, if a trifle superior, but they enjoyed talking to her, as she obviously relished the opportunity to practise her English. After their long and tiring walk, they decided to have dinner in the hotel and have a relaxed evening. They seemed to be the only residents in the hotel and the hotel owner seemed to have taken a liking to them and had decided to make their evening as pleasant as possible.

When she led them to the dining room, they noticed that there was a small bunch of flowers on their impeccably laid table. The light was muted, adding to the sense of intimacy. She served them a homely but superb meal, and, despite her occasional air of superiority, she did it with such grace that they were soon completely relaxed.

"It's been a wonderful day, James. I don't think I have enjoyed myself so much in a long time. Yesterday was great too," Maria said, as they were finishing their meal.

"I feel the same way, Maria. I'm so very glad we met yesterday. It's funny, but it seems like more time has passed than just two days. Time is such a strange thing. Some periods of time can go by so slowly, and others seem to fly by."

"Did you notice that we are the only people staying in this hotel? Just you and I, apart from the owner. I feel there's something rather special about that. I don't know whether you know what I mean."

"Yes, I do."

When they finished their meal, they were both ready for bed. It had been a good day for both of them, but also quite tiring. They walked up to their rooms on the first floor together. They reached Maria's room first. She turned the key in the lock of her door and opened it. She then turned back to face James, and said, "Thank you for a lovely day and evening."

He took her hands in his and held them by her side, and slowly inclined his head towards hers. She looked up and he could read the message in her eyes. Their heads got closer together until their lips met in a light brush.

Maria drew away at first, but then, a moment later, pulled James towards her and kissed him passionately on his lips. He responded immediately and they stood there for several minutes in the semi-darkness of the corridor. Then Maria released her hands from his and after drawing away, gave him one last kiss.

"Goodnight, James. That was a wonderful ending to a lovely day."

"Goodnight Maria. Sleep well. I will be thinking of you."

Chapter 19

He was up bright and early and went out to the balcony. It was another beautiful day, the sun was just rising over the horizon, and there was a stillness in the air. After he had showered and dressed, he went down to the conservatory to wait for Maria. He did not have long to wait as she appeared soon after, looking well rested. At this time of the morning, she wore little or no make-up at all, but he did not feel that she needed any, in reality, since she looked very good without it. In fact, he liked a more natural look.

Their host came to offer them breakfast and they enjoyed the simple, but very healthy fare on offer. James was thinking about their kiss the evening before and how quickly their relationship had bloomed since they had met, just two days earlier. He did not want it to stop there and wanted it to continue to progress, because he had not felt like this about anybody, ever before.

Maria was having similar thoughts. She too felt that their relationship had developed quickly and was pleased that she had met James. She seemed to be getting on so well with him, but then, she thought to herself, 'I have seen how people meet on the Camino, spend some time walking together and then get separated for ever, so maybe I should be careful before allowing myself to get too drawn into this relationship.'

They set off soon after breakfast. At first, the Camino followed a busy highway, and it was difficult to talk with the noise of heavy traffic going past them but soon, thankfully, it diverged, and they were back in the countryside and able to talk again.

"You know, Maria, we only met a couple of days ago and yet I feel I have known you for far longer than that."

"Yes, I do too."

"When I embarked on this Camino, I had a notion of what I was looking for and yet, now it seems to be taking me down a very different route."

"What do you mean?"

"I mean … meeting you."

"Are you sorry?" Maria asked.

"No, quite the opposite. Maria, meeting you has been wonderful, and I hope we can continue to walk this Camino together. We are both on our respective missions here but, maybe, we can fulfil these in each other's company, and with each other's help."

They walked on through the day. The final stage of their walk took them through a very lonely, wooded stretch of the Camino, where they saw absolutely no one else. At one stage, they passed by a monument and stopped to read the inscription on it. They were able to translate enough of it to understand that it was a monument to the fallen of the Spanish Civil War. Both had a broad knowledge of Spain's history, including the very turbulent period in the twentieth century. The Civil War of the nineteen thirties had divided the people and some of the scars of that bitter conflict were still present.

In the late afternoon, they arrived at that day's destination, the very small village of San Juan Ortega. They had to stay in the local *albergue* since there were no other options in this tiny village, but they were already planning to stay in a hotel when they got to Burgos the following day. The little village had only the one street, which was practically an extended square. It was lined with buildings on one side, including the little church dedicated to San Juan, another saint who cared for pilgrims and helped them on their passage. As they checked in, Maria asked the *hospitalero* whether there was a Mass in the church, and he replied that one would be starting in half an hour. She turned to James, and told him, "There's a Mass soon in the little church we just passed by. I would really like to go. Would you like to come with me?"

"Yes, I would. I went to a couple since starting, but I have missed them in recent days."

The little church was quite full, and they only just managed to find a place towards the back. The congregation was mixed, being mostly local inhabitants but there were also a few pilgrims like themselves. A small female choir sang throughout the Mass, which was a very simple and beautiful ceremony that moved them both. At the end of the Mass, the priest asked the congregation to move to the chapel next to the church. In that chapel, San Juan's body lay in an ornate stone coffin and there followed the now-familiar blessing of the pilgrims. After the ceremony ended, they walked further down the square.

"I am glad that we went to that Mass," Maria said. "I always find it so soothing, but tonight's service was particularly uplifting, especially with that lovely singing".

"I can't say that I am a regular churchgoer myself, but since I have been here, I have looked forward to going to these Masses, as they are so much a part of the whole experience," agreed James.

Their dinner in the *albergue* was a very simple one and, after they finished, they went back into the square and sat on one of the benches. The square was almost completely empty by then, and the only lights left were a couple of dim streetlights. Maria snuggled up to James and laid her head on his shoulder. They looked up at the sky. It was brilliant. Neither of them had ever seen the Milky Way shine as brightly as this. It was an amazing sight and they just sat there looking up at the sky, silently.

Chapter 20

He stood on the highest point of the hill, just below the wooden cross rising from a pile of stones. He had been told that this was similar to another, more important, cross that he would encounter further along the way, but the principle was the same. Pilgrims were meant to bring a small stone or pebble with them from their native country and deposit it at the foot of the cross. A fairly impressive pile of small stones had formed. Maria was walking up the hill some fifty metres further back. She joined him and they looked together at the great panorama below them. A nearby sign in Spanish announced, somewhat presumptuously, that this was the greatest view in the whole of Spain.

The hill they were on dropped down to the plain far below and, in the distance, they could see, albeit faintly, the city of Burgos. They had left San Juan in the early morning and had been walking steadily for a couple of hours. It had been a peaceful night for both of them, even though the albergue had been quite busy. This had been due, in no small measure, to the sense of peace that overcame them after their quiet evening sitting on the bench in the square, watching the stars.

As the started their descent down into the plain, it became

easier for them to talk. Maria broke the ice, saying, "That was a lovely evening yesterday, James. So very relaxed, just sitting beneath the stars. We take the sky so much for granted and never bother to look at it but, truth be told, with all the light pollution there is in Malta, we can very rarely see it the way we could last night. It's so beautiful when you can really see it!"

"Yes, that is so true. It's not surprising that the night sky, be it the moon or the stars, has always inspired poets, painters and musicians to great heights of creativity. Apart from the poetry it holds for artists and lovers the world over, I have always been fascinated by the grandeur of the universe. Cosmology is one of my favourite subjects," James replied.

"What exactly is cosmology? Is it anything to do with telling the future?

"No. You must be thinking of astrology," he said. "Cosmology is a science, whereas astrology is just a lot of superstitious hocus-pocus that many cheap magazines make money out of through the horoscopes they publish. Cosmology, on the other hand, is the study of the universe – its origin, its nature, and also its future."

"It must be a very interesting, but difficult, subject", said Maria with a sense of awe.

"That it is," replied James. "I am only a dilettante, of course, no scientist. However, I have read a lot written about it by authors like Stephen Hawking, Brian Greene and Carl Sagan, and find it so fascinating to learn where all that is around us came from, and what it is. I can get quite carried away by it. Some of my friends tell me that I should come down to earth, and maybe they are right, but the truth is that it raises such basic and important questions about the origin of everything that I cannot but read about it avidly. I also believe it lies at a confluence of science and a belief in a superior being, a creator."

"I had always thought that science and belief were somewhat incompatible," said Maria.

"Not necessarily. I believe they can coexist, even though science demands a rigorous discipline of testing hypotheses before accepting them. Well, one day, I will tell you all about it."

"I would love that, James," she replied, nodding emphatically.

Engrossed as they were in their conversation, they walked past the sign stating that they were entering the boundary of the city of Burgos without noticing it, soon found themselves walking through a park along a riverbank. They started to glimpse, through the trees, the twin spires of the city's great cathedral and soon, they were standing in front of the *Puente de Santa Maria*. It was a beautiful stone bridge crossing the river to the other side where there was a great gateway leading into the old city centre. They crossed the bridge, walked through the gate, and stood in awe at the scene that met their eyes.

The great cathedral rose from the square with a large and grand flight of steps on one side, while its twin spires reached up to the sky. The masonry work was an intricate pattern of lacework in stone, and the shadows cast by the strong sunlight created an almost unreal sense of relief. It was indeed a majestic sight. The square was full of people sauntering about, or standing in small groups chatting, while a group of children played on one side.

They had decided to stay in a hotel for the one night they were spending in Burgos, and they found one in the main square facing the cathedral. After checking in, they dropped their rucksacks in their respective rooms and headed straight for the cathedral. They knew they only had half a day to spend in this marvellous city and wanted to make the most of it. The interior of the cathedral was a revelation. They both felt transported and overwhelmed by its beauty and by the sense of history. Maria became so emotional that tears, which she could not stop, started to run down her face. Everything was so perfect! The stone tracery, the domes letting light into the space through the star-shaped stonework and the art pieces – paintings, sculpture and silverware. When James noticed that Maria was crying silently, he asked her with concern, "What's wrong, Maria? Are you upset about something?"

"No, it's not that at all. I am just overwhelmed by the grandeur and beauty of this place, and I became very emotional. It's a happy feeling, not a sad one."

"I can understand that. It is one of the most amazing churches I have ever seen," James concurred.

On their way out of the cathedral, they saw a small poster advertising a choir performance there that very evening. They stopped to read the programme, and Maria suggested that they have a look around the centre then go back there in time for the performance, a suggestion with which James immediately agreed.

They walked around the old city centre and then stopped in one of the bars in the Plaza Mayor to have a drink. They started a conversation with their waiter who told them all about the legendary El Cid, that city's most famous son. James recalled the 1960s film about the Spanish hero that he had watched on television some years ago. By this time of the early evening, the city had come alive, as Spanish cities tend to, since everyone had finished work and gone out for tapas and a drink or two before dinner. James looked at his watch and said that they should be heading back to the cathedral to get good seats. When they got there, they found that there were already many people, but they managed to squeeze into a couple of seats in the choir stalls very close to where the choir would be singing from.

The performance started on time. The choristers filed out and took their places in front of the great altar. Maria thought that they looked very impressive in their burgundy uniforms with the great, painted retablo behind them. When they were all in place, their director came out, bowed to the audience and, without further ado, led the choir into their first piece. It was one of Bach's chorales. The heavenly sound of their voices, combined with the superb organ playing, transported them both. The audience was also carried away and clapped enthusiastically after each piece. It was not just the music and the heavenly voices, but the whole experience within that magnificent setting, which made it so extraordinary.

When they left the cathedral after the performance, they were feeling quite overwhelmed by the experience and, not wanting to diminish it in any way, they found a very quiet little restaurant nearby, well away from the hubbub in the city. They wanted to continue cherishing the feelings they had experienced at the concert. They were almost the only diners in this small, intimate eating place, and since they were seated in one corner behind some large indoor plants, they felt quite secluded in their little niche.

"That was a truly wonderful concert," Maria reflected, as they sat down.

"It was indeed. I knew a good number of the pieces they sang, as I am quite a fan of Bach and Mozart. The choir was superb, and the organist was great too … and listening to the music in those surroundings was something else!"

"Are you keen on music then?"

"Very much so. I always wanted to play an instrument and sing in a choir but unfortunately, I've never had the opportunity to do so. My parents never considered sending me to music lessons. It's one of my big disappointments."

"I feel lucky. My parents, especially my mother, always wanted me to learn to play an instrument, and I went to piano lessons at an early age. Admittedly, at first, I found it really boring, but with time, I grew to love it so much. Once that happened, I practised regularly and managed to sit for, and pass, my exams. I still play and I am eternally grateful to her for having insisted that I take music lessons, God rest her soul."

"I guess you must miss her a lot. Has she been dead for long?" James asked.

"No, not that long, quite recently in fact," Maria replied, emotionally " … and, I do miss her, a lot."

"I lost both my parents some time back," he replied. "They were both great, in their own ways, but I lost them quite early on. I too miss them."

Maria put her hand over his arm, sympathetically. He looked at her, raised his other arm and stroked her face gently and tenderly and they stayed like that for some minutes, oblivious of the passage of time in their little corner of the world. They were generally aware of the other diners, but they had eyes only for each other just then. After a while, Maria said to him,

"We should be getting back to the hotel. It's getting late and we should try and make an early start tomorrow."

"I guess so. It's just that I didn't want to break the spell. I am having feelings like I haven't experienced in a long time, perhaps never," he said.

"Yes. Me too. But it's time for bed now, James. We can take up from where we left off tomorrow morning. It's not too long to wait, is it?" she joked.

"It's an age, uncounted centuries, eons … ," he joked back.

They walked back to the hotel, hand in hand, relishing the feeling of togetherness, the soft lights in the streets, which had now fallen quiet, and the great mass of the cathedral rising into the darkness as they walked past it. They let themselves into the hotel with the key they had been given. Apparently, everyone had gone to bed already and they went up the flight of stairs to their floor. When they got to Maria's room, she bent down to open the door and then turned back to face James. They stood there looking at each other and could see mutual desire reflected in each other's eyes. There was a tacit exchange of unexpressed thoughts, until Maria gave James a quick kiss on the lips and said,

"Off to bed now, James. We've had a great day together today, and we will have another one tomorrow, and the day after, and the day after that too, God willing – so there is time." She left the last phrase hanging in the air, with all the promise it held.

Chapter 21

The bells woke Maria up very early the next morning. They were so close to the cathedral that, when the bells rang to announce the first Mass of the day, she was immediately wide-awake. Thoughts flooded into her head, and she knew that she would never manage to fall asleep again. She thought back to the evening before, and to the few days preceding it. She realised that she was starting to feel something quite special for James, 'Was she falling in love with him?'

She really enjoyed being with him and talking to him and she also felt a very strong physical attraction, way beyond anything she had felt for any of her recent boyfriends or for Tom, for that matter, even though in the first year, things with him had been quite good. Then a conflicting thought arose. She hardly knew James. She had met him only four days before and she still knew so little about him. He seemed like a very kind, honest and upright person but she knew, from painful experience, that things were not always what they seemed. Yet, she felt that she did not want to shut herself off against a new friendship – which was rather more than a friendship, if she were to be honest with herself. 'I will let myself go with the current for the moment, and see where it takes me,' she thought to herself.

James too, was woken by the bells but he did not mind so much. He loved to lie in bed for some time before getting up to face the day. It was his 'thinking time' when, alone and very quiet, he could think about the day before and the day to come. He liked to think about what he had done right and what he had done wrong the day before, and how he could have done better. He would also think about the day that was just starting. He had always had a very organised mind, and loved to plan everything down to the minutiae, as far as he could.

He thought back to the last few days since he had met Maria just outside Logroño, and realised that he was becoming quite serious about her. He loved her company and he had really enjoyed walking with her. He also found her extremely attractive and sexy. Last night had been a dream! First there had been their tour of the cathedral setting a mood of otherworldliness, then the choir concert, which transported them yet again. Finally, their quiet, intimate dinner in the restaurant had felt as though they were the only two people in the world, dining alone in their little corner. When they had walked back to the hotel and stood in front of Maria's room, James recalled having an almost unbearable urge to make love to her. It seemed to him that she liked him, but she was clearly not yet ready to go beyond a certain point.

His remorse about the accident was still there. When it came to the fore in his thoughts, it could be quite painful and would render him almost incapable of functioning so, by way of self-preservation, he tried to keep these thoughts at bay, circumscribed, so he could keep them under control, as much as he possibly could. Thank goodness, he had thought less about it in the last few days. He thought back to Malta and wondered how Peter was getting on. He felt a bit guilty about not having called him in some time and determined he would do so that day. He also wondered whether the police had found out anything more about the accident. He hoped not and yet, in a perverse way, he almost wished that they would find him out, so he would have no choice but to confess it all and finally get it off his chest.

He thought about the atonement he had hoped to achieve. In all honesty, he was still not feeling that he was atoning for his crime to any significant degree. The Camino undoubtedly had some difficult and challenging moments, even hard ones at times but, overall, it had been enjoyable so far, so where was the sense of atonement? On the other hand, it had been uplifting and it had made him think about his life and how to improve it, especially now that he had met Maria.

He made his way down to breakfast and found Maria already there waiting for him. They sat side by side at the little table on the terrace, facing the sunlit square. The cathedral had already opened its doors and was receiving the first churchgoers. They ate in silence, enjoying the sun's warmth on their bodies and the peace of the morning. As they looked out over the square, they saw a large group of people congregating at the top of the large flight of stairs on the side of the cathedral and realised that it was a wedding party. There was the bride in her white dress and the groom looking very dapper in a grey suit. They were surrounded by a group of friends and family, and it was becoming noisier by the minute.

"Well, I guess we should be on our way and leave these happy people to get on with what they're doing," joked James, as they stood up and started to make their way out of the hotel.

They soon left the city well behind and after having climbed slowly for some distance, they found themselves on a seemingly limitless plain, and knew that they were in the *meseta*, a high plateau that stretched almost two hundred kilometres all the way to Leon, the next major city on the Camino. The sky seemed larger than life. They were able to see in every direction, over unending fields of wheat, punctuated by a few trees and a high range of mountains appearing dimly to the west. James reckoned that they must be the *Montes De Leon* and he was surprised that he could see them already from such a distance. It was a truly sublime sight.

They reached their destination for the day, the little village of Hornillos, quite late in the day, and were both very tired. Maria had developed some serious blisters on one of her feet, so they sat on a bench in the square, where she gingerly removed her boots and socks so that James could have a look. The nasty looking blisters were growing just beneath her toes. He lifted her foot on to his lap so he could take a closer look and work on them. He felt a thrill at this close contact. The blisters were hard to reach, but James managed to prick them with a needle that had been sterilised over a burning match. He then squeezed out the liquid from the blisters, before applying a Compeed patch over them. It was a painful process, but Maria felt a bit better after that, although she still limped as she walked the last few hundred metres to the *albergue*.

"I was afraid this would happen," she said. "A number of people I met warned me that, after a week or so, blisters often start to form. Let's hope this patch works. At the moment, I can't imagine myself walking another twenty-five or thirty kilometres tomorrow."

"I'm sure you will be much better tomorrow. The body has an amazing ability to heal itself and, with a bit of rest this evening, you should recover sufficiently."

After checking into the *albergue*, they sat on the terrace outside overlooking the little square. James was updating his diary, while Maria read her book. She wondered what had happened to Silvia. She had expected her to catch up after a day or two but there had been no sign of her, and the couple of times Maria tried to call her, there had been no answer. She hoped that nothing had happened to her. Maria had noticed, along the way, a number of little memorial stones, usually with flowers placed over them, to remember some pilgrim who had died along the way. With millions of pilgrims walking the way over the centuries, a few hundred must surely have died of illness or accident. Certainly, there had been some stretches where she could easily imagine someone tumbling off a precipitous path or, in more recent days, getting run over when the Camino crossed busy highways.

As the day drew to a close, they watched the beautiful sunset and then went back inside for dinner. There were a number of other pilgrims already seated in the refectory, waiting for the meal to be served. It was the usual simple fare, but very plentiful. They were sitting on a long trestle table with a group of mainly female walkers. The two sitting closest to them turned out to be two Brazilian ladies who were in Europe for the first time in their lives. As they chatted, Maria found herself loving their sing-song accent. It sounded very musical, and she loved the sound of Portuguese. Letitia and Rossana turned out to be very entertaining young ladies, and they told James and Maria all about the famous carnival in Rio, where they lived. They too were headed to Santiago and had been walking all the way from St Jean, but they had started before James had, since they preferred to take it at a more leisurely pace.

Before they knew it, it was 'lights-out' time, so they scrambled to their bunks and settled down for the night. James and Maria were sharing a double bunk bed. James insisted she take the more comfortable lower bunk, while he climbed up to the top one.

Chapter 22

When they went down for breakfast, the refectory was again quite full, but they saw the two Brazilian ladies sitting alone at one end and so they joined them. James asked them where they were heading, and they replied that they did not plan to walk too far that day as they too were having problems. Letitia's calf muscles were hurting her, so she would not be able to walk fast, while Rossana had developed some painful blisters. They had seen many pilgrims along the way who had stopped by the wayside to treat blisters, so they knew that this was an occupational hazard of the Camino. Letitia said that she had heard that the clinics in each village, which formed part of the Spanish health service, were very good and were geared up to help pilgrims with these, and other problems. Maria's blisters were a lot better than they had been the day before, and she felt ready to go.

They set off and, for a time, walked together. The two Brazilians talked about life in Rio, which they clearly loved. Neither James nor Maria had ever been to South America, but they were both familiar with Brazilian music. Maria reminisced about some Brazilian singers she used to love listening to in the past like Joao and Astrud Gilberto, Antonio Carlos Jobim and others. Then she asked them whether they could sing something Brazilian as they walked. Rossana said she would choose a famous one by the very persons Maria had mentioned and she and Letitia broke into song, as the four of them walked alone in the early morning. Maria had not heard 'The Girl from Ipanema' in a long time but it was one of her all-time favourites. The girls sang it very well and it was great to hear it sung in Portuguese, rather than in English. They walked on together for a couple of hours, but Letitia was clearly struggling to keep up and when they got to the little hamlet of San Anton, she told her walking partner, "I think we will need to stop for a bit of a rest, Rossana. My legs are bothering me and perhaps I should go to the *Centro de Salud* to see if they can do something for me."

"Would you like us to stay with you?" Maria asked.

"No, no, you must carry on. I may need to spend a few hours here and I don't want to hold you up. Rossana will be looking after me very well."

"Well, I hope we will meet further along the way then. Perhaps we'll come and visit you in Rio one day."

On that note, they parted company. Suddenly, Maria realised what she had just said. She had subconsciously linked herself to James, even if it were the sort of thing one would say, casually and in passing. She wondered whether James had noticed. She had often dreamed of going to South America, especially Brazil. To go there for the Carnival would be a real experience and she wanted to do it before she became too old for it. She wondered what the two Brazilians were making of Europe on their first trip outside their country. She had found them so lively and exhilarating and she hoped that they would meet again along the way.

"A penny for your thoughts," James interrupted her daydream. She realised that she had been deep in thought and silent for some time.

"Well, I was just thinking how I would love to visit Brazil someday. It was such fun meeting Rossana and Letitia, and I hope that we meet them again."

"Yes, very much so."

Then, he said, "Look, we're close to the next town. It's Castrojeriz, according to the map on the guidebook. Shall we stop there for some lunch?"

"Maybe we should just grab a snack and press on and eat it on the hoof. If we're hoping to get to Fromista tonight, we need to make good time, as we still have a long way to go."

"Yes, you're right," James agreed.

They walked through the day. Fortunately, the weather was kind, and it was not hot. There was a cool breeze blowing and there were enough clouds in the sky to shield them from the sun, as otherwise, there was little shade on the wide, open spaces of the *meseta*. They reached Fromista in the early evening and headed straight for the *albergue*. Maria's blisters were starting to bother her again and they were both exhausted after the long distance they had covered that day.

After showering and changing their clothes, they decided that they would take a short stroll to the nearby church of San Martin. Despite their tiredness, they did not want to miss seeing it. They had read that it was a beautiful eleventh century church, and one of the finest examples of Romanesque architecture in Spain, and they were not disappointed. It was breath taking in its purity and simplicity, and they spent some time just sitting in the pews, absorbing the atmosphere of the place.

As they walked out of the church, James took Maria's hand. She felt the warmth and strength of his hand over hers. Maria turned to James, saying, "Let's not have an *albergue* dinner tonight. I would rather be alone with you. Let's find a nice little restaurant like we did in Burgos."

"I was going to suggest the same thing myself. In fact, I looked up the guidebook and it highly recommends a place called '*Los Palmeros*.'"

They found it easily and, much to their relief, it was close. It was all they could have wanted, and more. It had a very welcoming, warm atmosphere with a timber ceiling, papered walls, carpeted floors, and a fireplace in the centre of one wall. The furniture was old, traditional Spanish, rather heavy, but it fitted in with the rest of the decor. They immediately felt very comfortable and very much at home in these surroundings. There was only one other couple in the restaurant. They looked like locals and were young and completely engrossed in each other, holding hands, and gazing into each other's eyes.

They ordered their meal and while waiting for it to arrive, they drank a glass of the local wine. It was a superb, aged *Ribera del Duero*.

"What a great place this is! It's just what we wanted," James remarked.

"Oh yes! It's perfect, so relaxing and so pleasant."

James took her hand in his and said, "Maria, meeting you has been wonderful. You are the sort of person I have always dreamed about but had never ever met until now. I was starting to give up hope that I would ever meet the person of my dreams and yet it seems that it has happened."

"You know, James. I feel the same way as well. I have been

thinking about this almost since we met a few days ago in Logroño. I must admit that, at first, my feelings were mixed with a certain amount of caution. I hope you understand. I was married before to someone with whom I thought I was in love. A relatively short time after we married, I realised that my husband was very different to what I had thought he was. It is as though he was projecting a certain persona before we married, and which then changed into something quite different. So, I guess I am a bit wary about new relationships. My last boyfriends have not given me much encouragement either, I must admit. With you, I feel it is different."

"I understand what you are saying, Maria, and I appreciate your sense of caution. I would not want to hurt you in any way, and you must take your time to decide how you really feel. I have already told you what I feel about you."

"If I were to follow my instincts, James, I know I am wholeheartedly for you. Perhaps, I should just follow them."

"You know, Maria, when I came on this Camino, I did it for a reason. There were certain problems in my life, which I wanted to try to come to terms with. I am not quite sure what I was looking for, but I never imagined, or expected, that it would be an opportunity for me to meet the person who may be the love of my life."

"And maybe mine too, James."

They left the restaurant much later, long after the only other couple had gone, and returned to the *albergue* in a state of euphoria.

The next few days were like a dream. They were completely engrossed in their developing relationship and, while they occasionally exchanged a few words with other pilgrims they met along the way, they only had eyes for each other. They seriously started to consider the prospect of a lifelong commitment, something they both yearned for. They talked about what they would do when they returned to Malta. And yet, with all the intimacy that was developing between them, neither of them felt quite ready to talk about their sense of guilt with the other. James knew that, at some stage, he would have to tell Maria about what he had done, but it still felt too soon to do so. Selfishly perhaps, he wanted their relationship to get even closer before he told her. On the other hand, Maria started to make tentative moves towards telling James about her own.

"I feel somewhat responsible for my mother's death and perhaps that is one of the reasons why I came to walk this Camino. I wanted to think about things, and I thought that coming here would give me the time and the opportunity to do that."

"Maria, you must not feel that way. When someone dies, there is always a tendency for the people left behind to feel responsible and to think that they could somehow have prevented it."

"Well, perhaps I could have," she said, but stopped short of saying more.

He thought to himself that Maria had little reason to feel responsible for her mother's death. He knew he had probably experienced the same thing when each of his parents had passed away, but that was so different from the guilt he felt now.

The Camino continued through the *meseta* for a number of days. They were now used to the flatness and the great open sky, the seas of cornfields and the huge flocks of sheep that they passed every so often. They stopped for half a day in the town of Sahagun to visit some of the many churches. Soon, they were approaching the great city of Leon at the western end of the *meseta*.

In one of their rare interactions with other pilgrims, they got into a conversation with Julia, a young German woman. They had started to chat after she asked them for directions and, within a short while, she was telling them all about herself. They sensed that she needed to talk, so James asked her why she was walking the Camino. Julia said that she needed time to think about the past but both he and Maria sensed that there was something she was holding back which, at the same time, she needed to speak about badly. They did not press her. A short while later, she reopened the subject herself and confided in them that her mother had committed suicide some months previously, and she was still trying to come to terms with it. She felt that she had not done enough to prevent it happening and still felt very guilty about this. She could not understand how her mother could have done such a thing, but she had to admit to herself that she had seen some of the signs of an impending crisis and now felt she had not done anything to prevent it happening, which was why she felt so bad about it. They both tried to comfort her, aware that she was crying silently. When she saw that they had noticed, she apologised for crying and blew her nose, looking embarrassed. Maria consoled her, saying that she should not feel bad about crying, since it was so important to release one's emotions.

She then empathised with her, saying, "Julia, I really feel for you. I too lost my mother very recently and feel a sense of guilt about it, thinking that I could have prevented it from happening, but you must not feel that way, because all too often, there is nothing we could have done."

Meeting Julia and hearing her story made both of them think back to their own feelings of guilt.

They reached Leon in the early evening at the end of a brilliant day. They walked through the uninspiring suburbs and were soon approaching the town centre. Suddenly, James stopped in his tracks and, turning to Maria, said, "Maria, there is the most amazing Parador in this city. I was reading about it in the guidebook. We have been roughing it for these last few days. How would you like to stay in the Parador for one night, my treat?"

"Are you serious? Can you afford it? It's bound to be very expensive."

"I'll manage. Let's do it."

"OK. But may I suggest that instead of booking two rooms, let's save money and get just the one," she agreed, with a suggestive twinkle in her eye.

Chapter 23

The Parador occupies what used to be the *Hostal de San Marcos*, a sixteenth-century building built to house the Military Order of St James. In the early twentieth century, it had been converted into a five-star hotel and was now one of the foremost Paradors in the chain. It was built around a large central garden with a marvellous cloister on one side, and a church on the other.

Maria and James stood in the square in front of it, marvelling at its beauty and majesty. They walked through the imposing entrance and went to the reception desk to ask for a double room. The receptionist greeted them, "*Buenas tardes, señores. ¿Quisieran ustedes una habitación doble?*"

"I am sorry, but we don´t speak Spanish," James replied. "We would like a double room, please."

"One moment. I will check for you," the girl behind the desk replied, switching to perfect English.

She spent some time checking but soon, she told them, beaming, "You are lucky. Someone has just cancelled. Otherwise, we would have been full. The room is on the second floor, and it overlooks the garden. My colleague will show you up to it now."

The room turned out to be a dream. It was very large, with a timber ceiling, a floor that was paved in beautiful parquet, walls partly panelled in wood and heavy, panelled wooden doors. The two big windows on one side let in a lot of light. The bed was massive with an ornate headboard and a canopy stretching out over the bed. The bathroom was no less impressive.

"This is great, James. Are you sure you can afford this? I didn't look at the room rates, but I'm sure it's very expensive."

"Let's not worry about that, and just enjoy the moment," he replied, smiling. He wanted, so badly, to make love to Maria there and then, now that they were alone in the room. However, he did not want to rush it and believed that neither did she. She had indicated very clearly that she too wanted to make love to him, but it would be such a special step that it was not to be rushed. So, he said, "Why don't we unpack our things, get our clothes properly washed and ironed, change into something clean and go down to dinner here? They're meant to have a great restaurant. We can then have an early night."

She immediately got his drift, and smiled, saying, "OK, dibs on the bathroom! We ladies need a bit more time than you men do to get ourselves ready. I guess we should at least try and look less like pilgrims in a place like this, if we can."

While Maria got herself ready, James looked out of the window. The garden they overlooked was a peaceful, green oasis in the city. It was very well manicured, without losing its natural look, and the green of the trees complemented the honey-coloured stone in the grand arcade that ran around all four sides of the garden. He heard Maria singing softly in her shower and listened to her in delight. It brought him back to thinking about their present situation, their being there together, sharing a room in this wonderful hotel. It had happened so naturally, and it was clear that they both wanted this. In fact, he recalled, Maria herself had suggested that they share a room!

Their relationship had grown so close in the last few days and, despite Maria's initial caution and reserve, and perhaps his own as well, he sensed that they were both ready for the next step, and indeed wanted it very badly. He could fathom that from the way they spoke to each other and from their body language. He knew how he felt when he was close to Maria or when they kissed. In the last few days, returning home from an intimate dinner, he always felt a great desire for her and it was apparent that she felt the same way. When they were staying in *albergues*, satisfying that desire could not even be considered, but tonight they were sharing a room and there was nothing to stop them.

Maria stepped out of the bathroom wearing the white towelling bathrobe that came with the room. She looked delightful with her sun-tanned skin, wet hair and the big smile on her face, and he had to make a big mental effort to stop himself from picking her up in his arms and laying her on the bed. Maria must have sensed it, and was smiling widely while she said, "Your turn now, James. Off you go for your shower, so we can go and get that great dinner you promised me."

As they descended the grand staircase to the foyer, they admired the tapestries hanging on the walls. The foyer was busy with a number of new arrivals checking in, but they saw no other pilgrims. One could easily tell who these were from their dress, the shoes or boots they were wearing and, of course, the inevitable rucksack and walking poles or stick. They walked into the central garden and the scent of orange blossoms hit them straight away. The sound of the water playing in the fountain lent a soothing feel to the garden and helped to cool the air down. They sat on one of the benches in a little arbour in one corner and were completely alone. James put his arms round Maria and pulled her up close to him. They half turned to face each other and before they knew it, they were kissing, gently at first, then hungrily. Both were completely engrossed, and it was only when they heard a polite cough, that they realised that they were no longer alone in the garden. A young mother was walking by with her child in tow. They released each other from the passionate embrace, feeling somewhat embarrassed at first, but as the mother and child walked on, they started to laugh.

"I think at our age we don't need to be sneaking kisses in little alcoves like this one," Maria said jokingly.

"Agreed. Let's go and get our dinner. I don't know about you, but I'm feeling peckish."

The restaurant was almost full, despite the relatively early hour. Probably, many of the guests were foreign, as it was far too early for the Spaniards to be having dinner. The waiter brought them the menu, but it was so extensive and there were so many unfamiliar items on it, that they asked the waiter for recommendations, and only then, ordered. While they waited, they looked around the restaurant. It was a grand room with a high, vaulted ceiling and more tapestries hanging on the walls. The lighting was soft creating a relaxed, intimate atmosphere, despite the fact that the room was quite full. They talked little while they ate, both thinking of what was to come. When they had finished their meal, James took Maria's hand in his and said to her, "Maria, it's been ten days since we met outside Logroño, and I feel my life has changed completely in this short time.

It's almost like another life has started. There are still personal issues I have, which I am still trying to come to terms with, but I feel that there is hope now."

"I feel the same way too, James. There is no longer any doubt in my mind that I have fallen in love with you, and I want nothing more than to express it in the most natural, and the most giving, way."

"I love you too. Although only a little time has passed, in some respects, it seems like an age, and I feel I have known you for a long time. Perhaps I knew you, deep down, even before we met, because you are the fulfilment of my dreams. You are the one person I always wanted to be with."

Maria pressed his hand tightly and said quietly, "Let's go to our room."

They left the restaurant and climbed the grand staircase to their floor. Maria felt like she was floating up the stairs. As they reached their room, James fumbled for the key, opened the door and as they entered, he pushed the door shut behind them, and they started to kiss passionately. The room was still in darkness, except for the moonlight entering through the Persian shutters on the windows, which allowed bands of light into the room. Maria put her hand on James's mouth, then took his hands and led him into the bedroom. They undressed slowly and letting their clothes fall to the floor where they stood. James gasped as he looked at Maria, who was now completely nude, facing him in the dim light.

"You are so beautiful, my love. I want you so much."

"I want you too, James."

James lifted her up in his arms and put her onto the bed and then climbed on to the bed himself and lay on top of her.

He felt like he had never felt before, an irresistible excitement coupled with a burning desire to become one with Maria, to envelop her completely, and to lose himself inside her. She felt his strength and wanted to surrender herself completely to it. She spread her legs and he entered her. They made love slowly and deliberately until they came together. As they did, James saw the look of bliss on her face that completed the ecstasy he himself was feeling. They lay like that for a long time just feeling each other's bodies and the warmth that spread between them. Then James moved to one side, and they lay side-by-side, facing each other and looking into each other's eyes. Maria stretched out her hand and gently touched the curl of hair on his forehead while he stroked her cheek tenderly and, in that position, they fell asleep.

Chapter 24

Maria woke up first. It was still dark outside, except for the moonlight that was filtering in through the Persian blinds. For a few minutes, she lay in that state of semi-consciousness between sleep and waking, until slowly she started to awaken fully. She felt a sense of peace, and clearly recalled her feelings of bliss just before falling asleep. She looked across at James and it struck her that neither of the two appeared to have changed their position since when they had fallen asleep. James was still facing her. He was sleeping peacefully, and his breathing was slow and regular. Occasionally, he made a slight moue, and she assumed that he must be dreaming. Soon, he too stirred and opened his eyes. At first, like she had been, he was in a state of semi-slumber, but then his eyes focused on her face and he looked at her for some moments.

"I love you, Maria."

"I love you too, James."

"I have never experienced such bliss and such peace as tonight."

"Me too, James."

They continued to lie like that for a few minutes until they were drawn inexorably towards each other again. They came together in the half-light of the early dawn, just as the birds started tweeting in the garden outside. Maria remembered the scene from Shakespeare's 'Romeo and Juliet' when the lovers woke up after their night of lovemaking and discuss whether it was the nightingale or the lark that was singing its song outside Juliet's bedchamber. Slowly the day came to life, as they lay on the bed whispering endearments softly to each other.

At seven, they rose from the bed and took it in turns to shower and get ready for the day, before going down for breakfast. The buffet breakfast was one of the best either of them had ever seen, and they indulged themselves, without going to excess. They sat close together at table and both felt a warm glow from the memory of their lovemaking and from their proximity. James simply could not keep his hands off Maria, either touching her arm lightly, holding her hand, or pushing a curl gently away from her eyes. He felt an insatiable urge to touch her. She returned his little caresses as far as she was able to in the crowded breakfast room. They both felt an enormous physical and emotional desire for each other while communing with their eyes.

Maria broke the spell first, and told him, "I feel so wonderful and so alive. I haven't felt like this in a very long time, perhaps ever. It's great to think that there are still so many days ahead of us on this Camino that has brought us together. I felt the wonder of each new day from the moment I started walking it but, since meeting you, I feel it very much more. There is the excitement of heading into the unknown, of seeing new places and experiencing new emotions and feelings. In fact, I am dying to start now but perhaps, before we leave León, we should try and see a bit of the city."

They started with the church of San Isidoro and then visited the great cathedral. The sun was shining brightly outside, so the stained-glass windows could be seen in all their glory, and glorious they were too. Neither of them had ever seen such magnificent examples. James remarked to Maria that even those of *Notre Dame* did not compare to the magnificence of these windows. The cathedral was somewhat smaller than that of Burgos, but it was perhaps a purer form of Gothic architecture, he thought, and somewhat less ornate and more austere.

When they left the cathedral, they walked through the *Barrio Humedo*, the old part of the city, which the receptionist at the hotel had recommended they visit. It was very much alive, even at that time of the morning, even though they had been told that all the open-air bars and restaurants would be full to overflowing with locals and tourists at night, with music playing in the streets and the little squares. They stopped at one of the bars for coffee and to plan their walk for the day. After considering the different options, they decided to walk up to the village of *Vilar de Mazarife* with a view to reaching Astorga, the next city on their route, the following day.

Once they had left the city, the countryside was beautiful, with gently rolling hills, well-tended fields and large clusters of the ubiquitous Eucalyptus trees, while in the background, but now much closer to them, were the *Montes de Leon*, which they knew they would have to cross in two days' time. It was there that they would reach the highest point in the whole of the Camino. Although it was not a very demanding walk, after some time Maria's calf muscles started to hurt. At first, she said nothing and tried to soldier on, but her pace slowed down, and she occasionally grimaced with the pain. James noticed, and concernedly asked her, "Is everything all right Maria? Are you in pain?"

"Yes. My calf muscles have been bothering me for the last couple of hours. It's never happened before. Maybe all the walking is starting to catch up with me, at last!"

"Let's have a bit of a rest and then we can decide whether to walk on or not."

"I would rather try and get to Mazarife now. We're not far off and I could go to the local *Centro de Salud* and check it out, but perhaps we can slow down a bit. I find that walking slower helps to ease the pain significantly."

"Are you sure, dear?"

"Yes."

Soon after that, they arrived at their destination. It was a very small village and there were no hotels or inns, so they had to go to the one and only *albergue* in the village. After they had checked in, they asked the *hospitalero* how they could get to the health centre, the *Centro de Salud*. He asked them what the matter was, and Maria explained. Pepe, for that was his name, gave her a big smile and told her she would not need to leave the *albergue* at all. He was, himself, a physiotherapist and he claimed to have helped countless pilgrims with their leg problems.

Maria looked at James somewhat uncertainly, but Pepe gave them no chance to refuse his help. He made Maria sit on a chair and pulled one up for himself, then picked up her leg placing it on his knee. He seemed to take the process very seriously. He kept exclaiming to himself as he manipulated her calf and leg muscles, suddenly expressing satisfaction when he reckoned that he had managed to get some muscle to behave.

After many grunts and sighs, Pepe seemed satisfied with his handiwork and said he was done. Maria asked him whether her calves would be all right and he assured her that they would be. James insisted on paying for the service, but Pepe said it was entirely *pro bono*, so James dropped some Euro notes into the little tip box on the reception counter.

The *albergue* had a dormitory and a couple of smaller four-bedded rooms, one of which they opted for, hoping that they would be alone. Pepe led them to their room, where they saw a rucksack already there, realising that they would have to share their room. They dropped their own rucksacks by one of the two pairs of bunks and then set off slowly to find somewhere to eat. They were lucky since there was a small tavern very close to the *albergue,* which seemed pleasant, so they walked in and sat down. The menu was somewhat restricted, but they noticed that there were two different types of paella. They had not had it for some time, and it sounded just like what the doctor ordered. They both chose a seafood paella and when it arrived, it looked wonderful. It was still in the heavy, flat pan in which it had been cooked, and was sizzling hot. While they waited for it to cool down, they drank a glass of the white wine the innkeeper had poured out for them. Soon, they were able to tuck in. The paella was way beyond their expectations, and they ate in silence, scooping one portion after another from the pan into their plates. James kept making little sounds of satisfaction as he ate.

"You really seem to be enjoying this, James," Maria remarked. "I don't blame you, mind you, because it's super. One of the best paellas I have ever eaten."

"It certainly is. I must say, we've had some good meals here in Spain. I was never familiar with Spanish cooking other than for paella, of course, but there is so much more to it than that. Do you like cooking, Maria?"

"I do, yes, but not as a daily chore. I enjoy cooking nice meals over the weekend, or whenever I have friends over, but otherwise my daily meals are very simple, mainly being salads, fish, the occasional pasta or risotto, lots of fruit and vegetables. I try to eat healthily. My one big failing is cheese. I simply adore cheese – the smellier the better. What about you, James, do you like cooking?"

"I am very much like you, I would say. Simple meals during the week when I am busy with work, but I too enjoy cooking something special over the weekend. I'm not much into meat, although I have a weakness for venison and quail. I have tried my hand at a few things, following Jamie Oliver, most of whose recipe books I have."

"Good for you!"

"Well, it looks like we will have to make some adjustments here. We both like cooking over the weekend and we both take short cuts during the week. We may have to be looking at a more coordinated effort, especially if we are to share the same kitchen," said James pointedly, while looking at her very intently

She looked at him for a few seconds before replying, saw him smile broadly and said, "Is that what I think it is?"

He nodded.

"Well, that must be one of the most unusual marriage proposals ever, my love. And my answer is ... YES!"

Chapter 25

That night, both of them got hardly any sleep. Maria thought back to James' proposal that had not been totally unexpected. They had grown very close in the last few days and it was clear that they were both ready and willing to commit themselves to each other. It had still taken her by surprise, however. She had not expected him to do it so soon, and in such an unusual way! Of course, she had learnt that he sometimes liked to approach things obliquely and there was a certain humour as well in the way he had put it. She had accepted with alacrity and told him that she did wish to share the rest of her life with him.

James thought about what he had done, and hoped that he had not jumped the gun, even though he felt that Maria's reaction had been positive. The thought of his guilt was never far below the surface, and it came to the fore again now, after he had made this commitment to Maria. He would have to tell her about it all at some time and, who knows what her reaction would be? Would she understand his inability to prevent the accident? Would she understand his panic at that moment? Did he himself understand it, his real motives? Had it been, ultimately, a selfish and cowardly desire to try at all costs to put the whole, terrible tragedy behind him? Then his thoughts changed and went back to their night in Leon and the great sense of joy it had given him, and the hope of a future, with Maria.

James climbed down from the top bunk and noticed that Maria was awake. He bent down to kiss her in her bunk.

"Did you have a good night, Maria?" he whispered, not wanting to wake up the third occupant of the room.

"Yes, I did but I spent a lot of time awake too thinking about yesterday."

"I did too. Do you feel any differently today, Maria?" he asked anxiously.

"No, I don't. I meant what I said yesterday when I accepted your proposal, even if it was pretty subtle, and you did not go down on one knee to make it", she joked.

They had a light breakfast at the *albergue* and set off straight away. It was very cold, but they knew from the days they had spent on the *meseta* that the temperature changed through the day. The mornings were often very cold, but it became very warm, and even hot, by the middle of the day. So, they would start off wearing three layers of clothing and, little by little, they would shed them one by one, until they were walking in just a tee-shirt and shorts. James asked Maria how her calves were feeling, and she said that Pepe must have performed miracles because she could not feel any pain at all.

Soon they reached *Hospital de Órbigo* and crossed the old stone bridge there. The Camino rose slowly over the next few kilometres, until they got to the stone cross on a vantage point high up, from where they could see the city of Astorga in the distance. It took them another hour to reach the city. As they walked through the old town, James said to Maria, "I missed you terribly last night in the *albergue*. Here, it will be no problem to find a hotel. In fact, I looked one up already. It's right in the centre and we will be there in a few minutes. Shall I book us in, Maria?"

"Oh yes! I want to make up for yesterday."

The Hotel Gaudi was in the main square to one side of the cathedral. It stood just opposite the *Palacio Episcopal*, which was named after its creator. It was one of Antoni Gaudi's lesser-known buildings but, nevertheless, a source of pride for the city. The hotel staff showed them to their room and this time they could, and did, not wait. They threw themselves into each other's arms and then on to the bed. They made love and time stood still. Afterwards, exhausted, they both fell into a satisfied sleep. When they awoke, it was the early evening. James was the first to awaken and he slowly touched Maria's brow. She had the most attractive eyebrows. They had struck him from the first time he had seen her. They were quite pronounced, but he found that extremely attractive and sexy. After a few minutes, she must have sensed his touch and opened her eyes.

"You have such sexy eyebrows," he said.

"What? My eyebrows? Is that what you like about me?"

"Yes, of course ..." he joked, " ... besides everything else, that is!"

"I must make sure not to have them trimmed then. Occasionally, I ask my hairdresser to trim them when I think they are getting too thick," she replied in the same jocular tone.

He continued to stroke her eyebrows, then slowly moved his hands down to her cheeks, and from there to her bare breasts. She pushed him away, playfully, "I think we have had enough lovemaking for one day. Let's go and get some dinner. I'm starving after all that exercise."

"OK, but I know for a fact that I am going to feel renewed after dinner and will want more of the same."

They went down to the restaurant, which was almost full, with quite a few pilgrims among the patrons. This hotel was in a different category to the Parador, where they had stayed two nights before, and more affordable for pilgrims. They called the waiter to order and he told them that they had a special menu that evening, featuring *Maragato* cuisine. He told them, in his clipped English, that Astorga was the main centre of the *Maragateria*, a people who defied classification. Some said that they were descended from the Berber tribes that had come to Spain with the Moorish invasion, while others claimed that they were descended from the Visigoths and their king, Mauregato.

He promised them that the meal would be different from anything that they had ever eaten, which indeed it was. The first course was a selection of ten different meats. This was followed by a dish consisting of beans, potato and cabbage, after which came a broth, and finally dessert. Apart from the way it was cooked and some unusual ingredients, the order of the courses seemed to be the very opposite of what they were used to.

"That was one of the most unusual meals I have had on this trip, and indeed ever," Maria said, as she wiped her mouth daintily with the white napkin.

"Yes, wasn't it? I felt it was strange to start with all those meats and end up with the soup but, in retrospect, it worked quite well."

"Well, as part of the coordinated effort in cooking that you proposed yesterday, I think we should agree to do this occasionally as a change from your favourite, Jamie Oliver."

"Hey, don't go ragging my hero!" he said, as they both

laughed.

James then looked Maria in the eyes, and said, "Let's go up to our room. I want to pick up where we left off this afternoon. I was so enjoying the story."

"Were you now?" laughed Maria.

The room was in semi-darkness, with only the light from the streetlamps that was making its way in through the louvered shutters providing any illumination. James switched on the bedside light, but Maria told him to switch it off again, "No, leave it James. We don't need it. I think that the light is just right. Very romantic."

She pulled him towards her and kissed him hard and once again, their passion overcame them and they tore each other's clothes off, falling on to the bed together. They made love, long and madly and when they were utterly spent, they just lay in each other's arms in the half-light, talking softly and caressing each other. They lay with their bodies wrapped together, feeling the warmth and the softness, and they fell asleep once again as they were.

Chapter 26

He awoke feeling a bit cold. They must have moved apart at night. The windows were open and there was a chill in the air. He covered Maria with the duvet and closed the windows. The sun was just starting to show itself. He knew that they had a long day of walking ahead of them and one that would prove tougher than any they had in the last ten days on the *meseta*. Today, they would start climbing the *Montes de Leon*, and by tomorrow they would reach the highest point of the whole Camino. He hoped that it would not be too taxing for Maria, and that her calves would not cause her any more problems. He spent some time looking at the sun as it slowly rose over the horizon and thought back over the last couple of weeks. So much had changed in that time and his walk in Spain had turned out to be so very different to what he had been expecting, at least in one important way.

What an amazing, and indeed, providential thing had happened to him! He had gone on this walk with a view to try to come to terms with what he had done and perhaps to find atonement, and ultimately, forgiveness. Instead, he had found what he was sure was the love of his life. It felt too good to be true and was certainly not something he felt he deserved, in the circumstances. Maria was all he could have hoped for, and more. Granted, they had only known each other for a couple of weeks and yet, in that time, he felt he knew a lot about her, and she about him, too. That reminded him that at some stage he would have to tell her his guilty secret. He wondered again whether she would understand what had driven him to do what he did. 'What if she didn't? What then?' The thought terrified him.

He heard Maria stirring and went back to the bed, kissing her as she came out of her slumber, "Good morning, sleepy head. You just missed a great sunrise."

"Well, what did you expect after all that lovemaking last night? I am still recovering. Don't forget that I am rather out of practice."

"That's great. I can coach you back to top form," he said, cockily.

They left the hotel with some regrets because they knew that they would have to go back to staying in an *albergue* at their next stop, as it was only a little hamlet, with very few facilities. However, it was the ideal jumping-off point to reach the pass over the *Montes de Leon* early the following day. At the top of the pass was the famed *Cruz de Hierro*, a small iron cross mounted at the top of a tall wooden pole. Their guidebook said that there were various theories as to its origin but what was certain was the fact that all pilgrims who passed it were meant to deposit a small stone or pebble from their homelands at its foot. While doing so, they were also supposed to say a prayer, or leave a written one attached to the pole. They had both brought along a pebble from Malta.

The path rose slowly as they climbed ever upwards through

little villages with very romantic names like *Murias de Rechival-do* and *Santa Catalina de Somoza*. They stopped for lunch at a small, simple bar in the little village of *El Ganso*. A large number of pilgrims had had the same idea, but they were able to get a table. While they waited for their order to arrive, James said to her, "One of the books I read about the Camino before I left Malta referred to 'the wild dogs of Foncebadon', our destination tonight. Its author explained that she had bought a device called a dog dazer to keep them at bay."

"What on earth is a dog dazer?"

"Well, apparently, it's a device which can emit a very loud, high-pitched sound that is meant to scare the dogs off. I was tempted to buy one but as I was trying to keep the weight of my rucksack down as far as possible, I decided to give it a miss."

"Well, you will have to look after me in Foncebadon once we get there. I love dogs but I don't fancy the prospect of wild ones!"

"Of course, I will, my darling."

Soon after lunch, they started to climb again until they reached the village of *Rabanal del Camino*, but after that the gradient increased and they found it necessary to stop and rest every so often. Finally, they reached their destination. The little hamlet of Foncebadon was quite small, with just a few houses, two *albergues* and one restaurant. After they had checked into the *albergue*, they threw themselves on to their respective bunks, since they were exhausted. They napped for a while and when they woke, they remained on their bunks for some more time, chatting across the aisle that separated them. It was the late evening before they both felt ready to make a move. They walked out of the *albergue* and wandered around the little hamlet, coming across some extraordinary buildings with thatched roofs. They asked one of the passers-by what they were.

"They are called *pallozas, señora*. They are very old, traditional buildings, very beautiful."

"Indeed, they are," agreed Maria.

The scene was magical. They were high up in the mountains and the clouds lay below them covering all the lower-lying countryside. The mountain rose to the pass that they would traverse the following day. An evening mist was starting to swirl up from the valley below, and the buildings and an ancient stone cross on a pedestal in the middle of the village had assumed a ghostly appearance. A couple of goats with long white goatee beards were nibbling at the grass in the half-light.

They sought shelter in the one and only tavern. The pilgrims' menu seemed to be the only option, so they took it, but it was actually quite good. It consisted of *Caldo de Gallego*, a Galician soup, followed by a nice portion of hake, and the inevitable caramel pudding, or flan, as Spaniards call it. They drank guardedly, as they were still quite tired from their climb up the mountain, and very soon after they had finished their meal, they headed back to their lodging.

"Well, Maria, quite a change from yesterday! Tomorrow, we will be back into a larger town and can stay at a hotel."

"You know, James, these periods of imposed abstinence only make me want you all the more."

"Do you want to continue to walk the Camino right up to the end or should we just drop the whole thing and go off on our own?"

"I think it would feel like a defeat at this point in time. I want to finish what I started. Don't you feel the same way too?"

"I think I do, yes," said James, frowning. "I too would feel very bad, at this point in time, were I to drop out of the walk, so I think that we should both finish it. We may never ever have another opportunity to do it again in our lifetime and, after all, it is what has brought us together. I believe it will continue to do so in the remaining days."

When they arrived back at the *albergue*, everyone else in the dormitory was already fast asleep. They undressed quietly and settled down in their bunks and were soon fast asleep. That night, James had nightmares in which Maria found out about his guilty secret, and that she was somehow inextricably tied up with the accident. He woke up, feeling preoccupied and sweating heavily. Maria seemed to be enjoying the sleep of the just, as she hadn't stirred at all.

It was still very misty when they left the *albergue*. In the half-light of the early morning, they could barely see where they were going, but the yellow arrows were there to guide them. Soon, they had left the village behind, and the path rose slowly but steadily uphill through the forest. The higher they walked, the more the mist dissipated.

After a short time, and without any warning, they found themselves in a clearing in the forest and standing in front of the famous *Cruz de Hierro,* the cross of iron. It was small, but it was attached to the top of a very tall wooden pole. At its foot, there was a large pile of small stones. At that time of the morning, there were already a few pilgrims standing in front of it with a reverential air. It was indeed a magical spot, and it was all they had read about, and more.

They walked up to it and started to climb the quite impressive pile of stones at its base. James wondered to himself how many pilgrims had passed by and deposited their stone to have created such a mound. Attached to the wooden pole there were letters, photographs, rosary beads and all sorts of symbols left there by pilgrims. They too had brought their own pebbles from Malta, and they placed them with deliberation, and somewhat reverentially, on the pile. They stood there, at the top of the hill, awed by the vista. James found himself praying silently that he could somehow be forgiven for what he had done, and that his love for Maria would develop into a life together with her and a fulfilment of what he and indeed, both of them, desired. Maria prayed that she could bring herself to accept what had happened to her mother and her role in it, and that her relationship with James would continue when they returned to Malta and would reach fulfilment in marriage.

Slowly, they walked down and stood there for some minutes, taking in the scene as other pilgrims went through the same ritual. Then, with a certain amount of reluctance, because they both had felt drawn to the place, they started to walk on. After a couple of kilometres, they reached the 'village' of Manjarin, which was described as having a population of one! It consisted, in fact, of a single building, a café, shop, museum and residence, all rolled into one. A multi-coloured signboard stood just outside of it, showing the distances to such diverse places as Jerusalem, Rome, Santiago, Machu Pichu and Mexico City.

They walked into the building and there they met the sole inhabitant of Manjarin, a colourful character who called himself 'El ultimo Templario', the last Templar. He was wearing the full regalia of the Knights Templar, including a white tunic with a big red cross on the front. He was busy describing, in broken English, the exhibits in his little museum to some other pilgrims.

They stopped to listen and helped themselves to a coffee. He knew a great deal about the Camino, and especially this particular stretch of it.

After they left Manjarin, the path descended steeply down to the little village of *El Acebo*. It was quite precipitous in places and James felt the familiar discomfort he experienced with heights. Maria seemed to be oblivious to this. In some respects, the descent was harder than the climb up, certainly more dangerous, because they both had to watch their step to make sure that they did not slip and fall on the loose stones that covered the path. When they finally reached the village, they sought out a place for lunch. Most of the few taverns were full, but they finally managed to find a table in one of them and sat down in relief. The walk so far had been exhausting, and they needed to recharge their batteries.

The little room they were in was full of pilgrims, many of them talking excitedly. Some had taken off their boots and left them outside, as was the custom, and they were trying to relax as best they could. Another couple had placed their arms on the table, rested their heads on them and were trying to sleep. James and Maria had spoken little while walking, as the difficult descent had demanded their full concentration, while the hard climb before that had left them out of breath, also making speech difficult.

"That was quite a walk," James remarked. "I really felt there was something very special at the *Cruz de Hierro*. When I looked at that pile of stones, I tried to imagine how many thousands, or even millions, of pebbles and stones it must have taken to create that mound."

"Yes, it was really very special, and it was hard to walk away from it. I was also really touched when reading some of the messages attached to the wooden pole beneath the cross. It is clear that many of the pilgrims who walk the Camino are doing it for very strong, emotional reasons."

"Indeed!" said James, thinking about his own.

There was a short silence after that, until Maria asked,

"Do we have much further to go till we reach our destination for today? I am longing to carry on from where we left off."

"Naughty girl," he replied, laughing. "Me too. Well, it's not too far now to Molinaseca. I was looking up places where we could stay there and found a really nice little hotel overlooking the river, so I shall ring them up and try to book a room straight away."

They reached Molinaseca in the early evening and found their hotel without difficulty. Their room was small and cosy with a welcoming air. It had a small balcony with wrought iron railings hanging out over the river, which flowed rapidly below. The sound of the water was noticeable.

"It's a really pretty room but I hope that we will be able to sleep with that sound," said Maria.

"I think you will probably find it soothing and relaxing. It's called white noise and it cancels out or masks any other sounds that could be more disruptive. In fact, you can actually buy small devices that generate white noise to help children fall asleep."

"Oh, I didn't know that. Hey, listen. Let's have an early dinner so we can come back here and sit on the balcony watching the river flow by."

"Ms. Mallen!" he said in mock seriousness. "I don't believe a word of what you are saying! You don't seriously think that

I really believe that you want to come back to watch the river. You are definitely trying to seduce me and, I must, say, I concede willingly."

She laughed at that and said, " … but not before dinner."

Chapter 27

James woke early as usual. Maria was still sleeping. He thought back to the night before. After the enforced chastity of the night before last, their last night had been a dream. They were starting to get to know each other sexually and each was beginning to understand what the other wanted and needed. They complemented each other in the giving and receiving of the bliss that their lovemaking created in them. James felt extremely protective towards Maria. He felt he wanted to envelop and protect her from all harm, and she too felt very protective towards him. She had sensed that, beneath his confident manner, something was bothering him. She could see it in certain moments when he would seem to go into a brown study, and he would stop listening to her, being engrossed in his own thoughts. She wondered what could be worrying him so much. She also felt a certain motherliness towards him, although he was a good bit older than she was.

When she awoke and they had prepared themselves for the day, they went down to breakfast. They sat at their table and tried to get as close to each other as they could. James could feel her thigh pressing against his and her hand resting on his arm. They both felt that they could have stayed on in their bedroom but, at the same time, they needed to continue their walk. They set off, and after a few kilometres, they passed through the city of Ponferrada. The route of the Camino took them past the stereotypical castle of the Knights Templar with its multitude of crenelated turrets. They crossed the iron bridge that gave the town its name and were soon back out in the countryside, heading into the Bierzo region. Their destination that day was, in fact, *Villafranca del Bierzo*, the old capital of the region. It was a relatively easy walk, although quite long, and they reached their destination in the late afternoon. James had looked for a hotel and the only one that had any rooms available was called *La Puerta del Perdon*. From his very limited knowledge of Spanish, he knew that this meant the door or gateway to pardon, and he wondered whether there was anything significant or symbolic about this.

Villafranca turned out to be a delightful little town. After checking into their hotel, they went for a walk round the town. They soon found themselves in the *Plaza Mayor*, a lovely square. They sat down at one of the cafes and ordered a glass of the local Bierzo white, which went down very well. They were both feeling very relaxed as they watched people go by. The atmosphere was laid-back, and no one seemed to be in a hurry to get anywhere. Maria had been thinking that perhaps the moment had arrived for her to confess to James her reason for walking the Camino. They had become so close that she no longer felt able to conceal this from him so, after a while, she launched herself into it.

"James, I believe I told you how touched I was by some of the messages I saw attached to the *Cruz de Hierro* in some of which the pilgrims gave their reasons for undertaking the

Camino."

"Yes, I remember you saying that. I was quite touched myself, actually."

"Well, I have a little confession to make. I had another reason for coming to walk the Camino, as well ..."

"What was it?" asked James, curiously.

"I will tell you. It's about my mother," she began hesitantly, knowing this was going to be difficult for her. She did not feel she could just come out with it and felt the need to first explain what had led up to the accident. So, she went on, "My mother suffered from Alzheimer's Disease, and my sister and I used to take it in turns to look after her as she was still living at home. She wasn't yet a very bad case, so she could still live at home, but needed to be watched all the time. One day, when I was supposed to be looking after her, my then boyfriend called me and we ended up having a big argument over the phone, which was when I broke up with him ..."

She paused for some moments. Her heart was thumping hard at the memories that were being evoked by the narration.

"Yes, and so?" James prodded gently.

"The fact is that my mother did not like my boyfriend and since I did not want her to hear me speaking to him, I went to take the call from the terrace at the back of her house."

"OK. That's understandable."

"Yes, but I spent a good twenty minutes on the phone and when I eventually hung up, I went back to the living room where I had left my mother watching television, but ... she wasn't there."

"So, where was she?"

"Well, at first, I thought that she had gone up to her bedroom to sleep, so I went upstairs to see how she was feeling, but she wasn't there either. Then, I looked in the other bedrooms and the bathroom, and there was no sign of her anywhere. I had noticed before going upstairs, that the front door was open, but had not given it much importance since I thought that it had probably been my mother's nurse who might have left it open as she left, after I relieved her. Anyway, when I didn't find my mother anywhere in the house, I realised that she must have walked outside, so I went to look for her.

At first, I couldn't see anyone, the street was deserted but then, when I walked in the other direction, I found her lying on the ground. She was partly on the pavement and partly on the road and I realised that she had been hit by a car, as she was bleeding badly. I called for an ambulance, which came quite quickly. I went with her to the hospital, but they couldn't do anything for her. Her injuries were too serious, and she died a few hours later. The fact is that I felt responsible for her death. Had I been with her, instead being on the phone for so long, none of this would have happened. I have not stopped blaming myself. Of course, I also blame the driver who hit her and did not even bother to stop but just drove away, leaving her there to die. If I could find him, I would kill him!"

James went cold.

Oblivious to the reaction that her story had set off in James, Maria continued, "For a number of weeks, I was feeling really down, with a huge sense of guilt. Then, a friend of mine told me about the Camino and suggested that it might be a way for me to try to come to terms with what had happened. In fact, we were going to walk together but she had to cancel at the last minute because of some family issues. Therefore, I ended up coming on my own, which is just as well, because I might never have met you otherwise."

"What was your mother's name?" asked James, in barely concealed horror.

"Her name was Antonia Pace. Maybe you read about the accident at the time. It was in all the newspapers."

James mumbled something about vaguely remembering. His mind was in turmoil. His world had just collapsed around him. He recognised the name of the old lady whom he had knocked down that night. At the time, he had never managed to read the article in the newspaper to the end, due to a sense of horror at what he had done. Therefore, he had no inkling of what the names of his victim's daughters were. Maria, whom he had fallen in love with and who had fallen in love with him, was one of the two daughters! Horror of horrors! He could not believe it. What was he going to do? For a few moments, he could not bring himself to speak, hardly being able to breathe, but then, with a big effort, he said, "I am so sorry to hear this, Maria. What a terrible shock it must have been, but you must not blame yourself for a moment. It could have happened at any time, and in different ways."

"But I still feel so bad about it. In these last weeks since we met, thank God, I am slowly coming out of the depression I was suffering, and am learning to come to terms with it."

He felt his heart racing, and thoughts flooded his mind.

'Oh God! Oh God! What am I going to do? This is unbelievable and terrible. How can Fate be so cruel? I found the love of my life in Maria, and she is in love with me. Now I find out that I am the very person she probably hates above all others. She said that she could kill the person who ran over her mother and left her where she fell. If I were to tell her, she would lose all faith and trust in me, and her love for me would turn into hate. I couldn't bear that! Oh God. What a nightmare! Do I *have* to tell her? Can I not try to atone for it on my own, without ever having to tell her, especially as I now know whom I have hurt? How would that be? She would continue to believe in me, and our love would continue. Yet it would be a sham. How could I not tell her? Even if she never found out, I would always know that I am the one who killed her mother. I would know that I was the person she hated, whilst living with her, when making love to her. I would bear this guilty secret all through my life. I cannot do that! I would be living a lie. I want to tell her the truth and the whole truth, unadorned, but I do want her to understand at least, that I could not have prevented the accident even though, had I been going slower, the impact may have had a less severe result. I need more time to think but I must tell her tomorrow at some stage, before the end of the day.'

While he was deep in thought, Maria had ordered another round of drinks, which had just arrived at their table.

"Let's drink to us, James. To our future happiness."

"To our happiness, my darling. There is nothing I want more," he replied wistfully as he took her hand, squeezed it hard and he went on holding it.

They sat there well into the evening, dining on tapas right there in the square. Maria was in a talkative mood and kept the conversation going almost singlehandedly. James felt thankful because he would have found it very difficult to participate actively. He nodded at intervals and made the occasional remark. Maria was recounting the hard time she had gone through after her mother's death, her friendship with Greta, their plans to walk the Camino together and how these failed at the eleventh hour, when Greta had to bow out.

As she chatted, Maria realised that James was far less talkative than usual. She thought to herself that he seemed to be unusually thoughtful, and even morose.

"You're very quiet tonight, dear," she said.

"Sometimes my demons come back to haunt me. During the Camino, and especially since we met, they have rarely shown their faces but occasionally they do."

"Is it something you want to talk about, James? I want to help if I can. We all have problems of one kind or another, but I really believe that a problem shared is a problem halved."

"My darling, I shall talk to you about it, but not tonight. Tonight, I want to make love to you like there's no tomorrow."

"That's what I want to do too, even though there will be many more tomorrows – indeed a whole lifetime of them."

Chapter 28

James awoke with a sense of foreboding. It was pitch dark outside. He could hear Maria breathing softly beside him. For a few hours, he had managed to find oblivion in sleep. He recalled how they had made love. Unlike previous times, last night, his lovemaking had an element of desperation. He really felt that it would be his last time and, like a condemned person eating his last meal, there was something unreal about it. He realised that Maria must have sensed it as she looked at him quizzically a couple of times, although not saying anything.

He lay awake thinking about how he would tell Maria about his involvement in her mother's death. He was terrified at the prospect. Although he knew she loved him, as he loved her, yet he knew that, in her mind, he would become a most reviled person. Would she ever understand, and would she ever forgive him? The thought that she might not was painful in the extreme. He could not bear the thought that, having found his loved one, he could lose her again after such a very short time.

Time passed slowly but, little by little, the day dawned. As light flooded into the room, Maria stirred and awoke. As she saw him lying near her with his eyes open, she stretched out her arms, cuddled up close and held him tightly. He responded by kissing her on her face and on her lips.

"Are you alright, James?" she asked him. "You seemed different last night while we were making love. You seemed to be worried about something or other. I can tell. If there is anything I can help you with, please tell me."

"Yes. I shall. Just remember that you have become the most important part of my life," he said, with a serious look on his face.

"I know that James, and you have become mine."

They got out of bed then and prepared to leave. Soon they were on their way, as they had a very hard day ahead of them. Having descended from the *Montes de Leon* just two days earlier, they now had to climb the next range of mountains in their path, the *Cordillera Cantabrica*. They were headed for the little village of *O'Cebreiro* at the top of the pass. It would be an almost constant climb all the way. James had already more or less decided to speak to Maria after they got to their destination. He felt he needed the whole day to think about what he was going to say, and how he was going to say it.

It was barely light when they left and it remained quite dark as they were walking through the deep Valcarce valley, following the river. They stopped for breakfast in the small village of Trabadelo but pressed on after that, as they wanted to make as much progress as possible before the midday heat. The road they were following soon turned into a stony path, which was very steep and continued rising implacably. As they neared *O'Cebreiro*, the view down the valley was stupendous.

They climbed the last couple of hundred metres and, as they turned a sharp bend in the path, they found themselves entering the village. *O'Cebreiro* struck Maria immediately.

There was something so attractive about it that she could not at first quite put her finger on. Then she realised that it was partly the homogeneity of the place. The walls of the houses and of the little church and the paving of the few streets were all built out of the same stone. Another factor was its location at the very top of the pass, with great sweeping views in all directions. The one main street through the village was full of pilgrims walking through it.

They headed to the only hotel in the village, and went in. The receptionist greeted them in English, and they asked her for a room, only to have her tell them,

"I am so sorry, *señores*, we booked our last room just a few minutes ago. We are full up now. The only thing you can do is to try the *albergue*, but better hurry, because many pilgrims have arrived here today, and they too may be fully occupied."

They thanked her and hurried to the nearby *albergue* to ask for a couple of beds. The *hospitalera* consulted her chart and told them that "The *albergue* is full tonight but we have opened up a small annexe and we can offer you a couple of beds there, if that is all right with you." "Well, we don't have much choice," said Maria. "Yes, of course, we will take them, *señora*, many thanks for helping us."

She accompanied them to the little annexe next door. The dormitory was not very large, maybe ten beds in all, most of which seemed to have been occupied already as there were rucksacks standing next to the bunk beds. They picked two of the few remaining bunk beds and, as usual, James let Maria take the lower bunk. After they had showered and changed into fresh clothes, they met in the entrance of the *albergue*.

"What would you like to do now, James? Shall we go for a

walk around the village before dinner?"

"Yes, let's do that," he replied, in a subdued voice.

They walked up the main, and indeed only, street of the village. It was remarkably small and exuded an atmosphere of warmth and hospitality. There were a couple of small shops and a tavern or two. At the top of the street, there was the little church they had passed on their way in. It had a small parvis enclosed by a low wall built out of the same stone as everything else. They walked in, and Maria was immediately struck by what she saw. The church was in semi-darkness. At the far end was the altar and, over it, was a crucifix in a naïf style, which was very touching. There was soft choral music playing in the background. The quiet, the flickering candles and half-light should have provoked a great sense of peace, which it did for Maria. However, James was in turmoil at that moment. He was terrified about what was to come soon.

On an impulse, Maria went up to a lady sitting in the pews and asked her whether there would be a Mass there, that evening. The lady spoke no English and did not understand what Maria was asking, but a man who was sitting close by and noticed what was going on, interceded,

"*Señora*, may I be of assistance?" he asked.

"I was trying to ask the lady whether there is a Mass here tonight."

"Ah, I see. Yes, there is a Mass at seven o'clock. I would suggest that you come early because it is always very popular. Apart from the local residents, many of the pilgrims who are sleeping over in the village attend as well."

"Thank you *señor*. You are very kind."

She turned to James and said "Let's come to the Mass tonight. I really feel I need and want it, especially in this wonderful little chapel."

"Yes, my love. I too feel that I want it and need it. Well, it's not far short of seven and I would suggest that we stay here until the Mass starts."

"I agree. Let's do that."

They sat, side by side, very close together. Maria was transported by the atmosphere and felt very emotional. She remembered why she was there and all that had happened since she had embarked on the Camino, and thanked God for this, praying that all would go well. James was in turmoil with a multitude of different, conflicting feelings. On the one hand, he felt so much in love with Maria, but he knew that in a short while he was going to have to tell her all and was terrified at the prospect of her reaction. He, too, sensed the peace and serenity that the place inspired and yet, this was being overshadowed by the fear and dread he felt.

Soon, a bell rang to announce the start of the Mass. Meanwhile, the church had filled with people, and it was now quite full. Everyone participated in the service in a heartfelt way and, once again, the priest called up the pilgrims for a special blessing at the end. Maria and James stepped forward to join the other pilgrims by the altar.

As they left the church, James felt his entrails churning with the tension he was feeling but he knew that the time had come. As they walked behind the church, he noticed a bench that was quite secluded among the trees. He pointed at the bench, saying, "Maria, let's go and sit on that bench. There is something I need to tell you."

She looked at him quizzically, noticing the tension in his

voice. They sat down together, and she noticed that, this time, he did not put his arm round her shoulder as he usually did but sat with his fingers interlaced together and his arms resting on his knees, while looking down at the ground.

"I, too, came to walk the Camino for a reason, Maria. It's something which I have been wanting, needing, to tell you for some time since I have come to know you and love you. However, after what you told me yesterday, I must do it now. I came because I had a great sense of guilt and hoped that I would find a way to atone for something I had done, and perhaps even to find forgiveness. Instead, I have found love. I have found the one person I want to spend the rest of my life with and yet, to do this, I must do something that is going to be very painful for both of us."

Maria listened in silence.

"Some months ago, I had a very bad day at the office. Everything went wrong on that day and the last straw was a big argument I had with one of my top clients, someone with whom I always had a great relationship. I left the office much later than usual and was dying to get home to try to put it all behind me. Usually, I drive home along the coast road, because I love the sea and find it relaxing. On that occasion, however, I was in such a rush to get home that I took the more direct route. I was driving faster than usual too. As I rounded a bend, someone suddenly stepped right in my path. I slammed the brakes on. As I did so, I realised that it was impossible for the car to stop in time and my car hit the person crossing the road.

"Although, my car had slowed down almost to a halt, it was still moving. I realised in that moment that the person I had hit had fallen to the ground and saw that it was an elderly lady. I don't know what came over me: I just panicked, I completely lost control of myself, I saw my life in ruins. Before I knew it, my right foot came to rest back on the accelerator pedal and my car just moved away from the scene of the accident as though without my volition."

"Oh, God! No, no, no…," exclaimed Maria in horror, her hand going to her mouth.

James went on as though he had not heard, "I tried to persuade myself that it could not have been too serious and that she would be found and taken to hospital. The next day I read in the papers that she had died of her injuries and the full enormity of what I had done, hit me."

"My mama. My poor mama."

"When you told me yesterday about your mother's accident, I nearly died. How can fate be so cruel, that it should have to be you? Or is it, perhaps, poetic justice? Perhaps this is what I deserve. I can imagine how you must be feeling. Maria, I am so very, very sorry. I know that nothing I can say will change anything. Nothing will bring your mother back to life or turn the clock back. I wish I could do that more than anything in the world, believe me! I hope that …"

The look Maria gave him cut right through him and he stopped in mid-sentence, as she let loose at him,

"How could you do that? How could you leave her lying there? How could you? I thought I knew you. I thought the world of you and now this! I too wanted to spend the rest of my life with you but how can I now?" Tears were running down her cheeks and falling onto her shirt.

"What can I say or do to ask for your forgiveness? I would do anything, anything at all!"

"I need to be alone. Leave me alone. Go!"

She was sobbing uncontrollably. As he moved to put his arm around her to comfort her, she pushed him away, "Please, go, go!"

Chapter 29

He left the church in utter despair and stumbled out of the little garden behind the church, walking on out of the village. He felt he had to do push himself physically to try to assuage the enormous emotional distress he was experiencing. He walked around the road that circled the village several times because it was too dark to venture any further than that. While he walked as hard as he could, his mind was in turmoil with thoughts chasing each other around his head,

'It went even worse than I had imagined! Maria was, understandably, extremely upset, and has lost all faith in me ... She will never want to see me again. ... I have re-awakened the pain she had suffered with her mother's death ... Could I have done it differently? Shouldn't I have been more circumspect and gentler? But whichever way I told her, I know that the result would always have been the same ... I had not even dared to try, at least, to justify my inability to avoid the accident as I had planned to do ... What am I going to do now?'

Perhaps, Maria would be ready to talk to him later, or the next day. He would try and talk her through what he had done and how it had happened, and try to get her to understand his actions, when even he himself found it difficult to understand them. Despite everything, he still did not regard himself as a bad person. Perhaps he could restore her faith in his essentially good nature so that she might see what happened to him as an aberration, the result of a moment of panic and fear. Would that make it any better? She would probably never get over the fact that he had left her mother there, badly injured, dying and vulnerable. It was unforgivable.

After some time, he walked back into the village and returned to the garden behind the church. Maria had gone. He caressed the back of the bench where she had been sitting as though that would conjure her up, but it was just hard, unyielding wood. He walked down to the *albergue* to look for her, but she was not there either. It did not take him long to search the single street in the village and to see that she was nowhere around.

He went into one of the taverns, sat at a corner of the bar and ordered a double whisky, neat. He downed it in one gulp and ordered a second. The raw spirit went straight to his head in a few minutes and his pain started to dull slightly. The tavern was full of people, but he could not face the idea of talking to anyone else. He just sat there in his corner and drank until he numbed his sense of despair and was practically oblivious to what was happening around him. He must have fallen asleep at the counter because the next thing he knew, he was being shaken awake by the barman.

"*Señor. Señor* … we are about to close for the night. Go to wherever you are staying but be careful! Do you need someone to come with you?"

"No, it's all right. I'll manage," James slurred as he got up. He was barely able to stand but, with a big effort, he tottered to the door of the tavern and stepped outside. The cold hit him hard. The temperature must have dropped enormously, which was to be expected up here in the mountains. He staggered to the annexe of the *albergue* where they were staying and made his way in as quietly as he could. The dormitory was in darkness. Carefully, he groped his way to his bunk. To his relief, Maria was there in the lower bunk, fast asleep. He spent some minutes looking at her and wondering whether he could somehow project his thoughts, his longing, to her in her sleep, then he shook his head in the darkness. He undressed and climbed up to his bunk and lay down. His head was spinning. He lay down, utterly spent, physically and emotionally. His tiredness, and the alcohol, finally got the better of his emotional state and before long, he was fast asleep.

He woke many times through the night, mainly as a result of some very disturbing dreams, fuelled further by the excessive quantity of alcohol he had consumed. He flitted between sleep and wakefulness and, each time he awoke, the physical and emotional pain hit him. It was one of his worst nights ever. At five in the morning, he gave up trying to sleep again and just lay on his bunk thinking. He would wait until Maria woke up and then he would try to speak to her again. He would explain to her what had happened and how it had been, perhaps she would begin to understand, and maybe, just maybe, she might start moving to forgive him. It pained him enormously to think that the one person he had ever felt closest to, and loved with a passion, now probably hated him.

The dormitory started to come alive as the day dawned and he watched Maria from his bunk above her. She was still sleeping, and he was surprised that she had slept through the night. He would have thought that she would be too upset to sleep, like he had been but, perhaps in her case, the emotional stress had exhausted her. He was glad that she had not experienced a night like his. Soon she started to stir slowly. She was sleeping on her back and as she awoke, she was looking straight up. As she opened her eyes, she found herself looking up at James on the bunk above her. At first, her look had the same gentle expression of previous days, and for a moment, he had a brief spark of hope. However, as she became fully conscious, he could see her expression change almost in a flash. Her eyes focused on his and he saw the gentleness transform into hostility.

He climbed down quickly from his bunk and knelt by her bedside. He did not dare touch her, but he held his arms out to her, pleading,

"Maria, please forgive me. I want you to understand that I could not have prevented the accident. I know I was driving faster than I should have been but even were I to have been driving slower, there was no way I could have avoided hitting your mother. At least, I want you to understand that. As for the rest, as for leaving your mother there, I have no excuse to offer because there is none. I am completely to blame for that. I still don't know what came over me but, whatever it was, it was selfish and cowardly, and I can never forgive myself for that. Can you forgive me, Maria, can you?"

She looked at him with an expression that he had never seen on her face before and said nothing at first. Then, she sat up in her bed and said,

"James, I am really upset. At the moment, all I want to do is to be alone to think about all that has happened. It would be best if we went our separate ways, at this stage."

"Please, Maria. I can't be without you. I want you. Let's try and resolve this together."

She got out of her bed, picked up her towel and went to the bathroom, leaving him standing there. He sat on her bunk bed felling her warmth on the bedclothes, stroking the hollow in her pillow where her head had rested.

He waited, but she did not return for some time. He packed his rucksack, ready to leave, and kept on waiting. Eventually, she came back, packed her things, laced her boots and walked out of the *albergue* without saying a word. He followed her at first, but she walked on determinedly without looking back, just striding ahead, following the yellow arrows.

He followed her at a distance, always trying to keep her in sight without getting too close. It was a very misty morning, and there were times when he could barely see her ahead of him, increasing his fear of losing her. So long as he could keep her in sight, he felt that there was a thread joining them; that there was still hope but he feared that, were he to lose sight of her, he might lose her forever. He realised that he did not even know where she lived in Malta. During their lightning court-ship, they had never exchanged addresses.

The path followed the ridge at the top of the mountains for some kilometres. When she stopped after a while at a roadside bar for a snack, he stopped too. She sat down at a small table for one. He sat at another table and watched her as she ate her sandwich and drank a coffee. Although he did not feel like hav-ing anything, he ordered a coffee perfunctorily. She sat alone and her body language made it clear that she did not want to talk to anyone. Most of the time, she just sat there, staring into the distance. He wondered what she was thinking.

He sat there, yearning to get up, go to her table and talk to her and yet, he could not. She had said that she wanted to be alone to think. Maybe it would be better if he gave her this space. He certainly did not want to alienate her any further. He would continue to follow her from a distance, never letting her out of his sight and, as soon as he felt that he could approach her, he would do so straight away. In the meantime, he was really suffering at the thought that this might never happen, and that he would lose her for good.

After a while, when she had finished her snack, she got up, hoisted her rucksack onto her back and left the tavern, with her scarf round her neck. Her slim figure seemed to him to be so vulnerable beneath her massive rucksack. He longed to be next to her, to hold her, conversing as they had done for so many happy days, but he now felt excluded and ostracized. He had never felt so bad.

When they reached Triacastela at the end of the day, he wondered whether she would stop there, as the guidebook suggested. He was still following her at a distance. When they entered the little town, she headed towards the *albergue* and checked in there. He waited until she had completed the process and then checked in himself. There was no hot water, so he had to content himself with a cold shower, then he went to put his clothes in the washing machine. Once he was ready, he looked around for Maria, but she was nowhere to be seen. She must have left the *albergue* while he was showering.

He also went out and walked through the one main street looking for her. There were a few restaurants with tables outside, but he did not see her anywhere. When he was about to give up, he saw her at one of the outdoor restaurants just off the main street. His heart jumped. He went up to her, and with a beseeching look, he pleaded, "Maria, may I sit with you, please?"

She nodded almost imperceptibly but looked away as he sat down.

"I am going crazy without you. I had a terrible night, and I cannot stop thinking about what I have done and what it has done to you, and to us. Please, please understand that I will never stop blaming myself for my terrible moment of weakness and cowardice. I know that I have taken your mother away from you forever. Can't you ever forgive me? I know I cannot live without you. I have found love and I am sure that you have too. The person that has fallen in love with you and the one you have fallen in love with are the real me. I don't know that other person who, that night, left your mother lying on the road."

"How can you say that?" she said, crying softly. "We are all responsible for what we do. We can't just disown something we have done. I know how I feel about you, but this has made me doubt everything. I need time to think, and I need to do it on my own. Please leave me alone."

He nodded sadly, got up and walked away.

Chapter 30

She sat there alone for a long time after she had finished her meal. She had picked at her food with little appetite but then asked for a half bottle of wine, which she nursed for the next hour or more as she mulled over all that had happened in the last twenty-four hours. She was deeply troubled. In the relatively short time that she had known him, she had fallen deeply in love with James. There were so many things she loved about him: his kindness, his intelligence, his caring for her and concern for others, and his calm. She found him so interesting to talk to and so knowledgeable about many diverse subjects and always ready to listen, such a rare quality, since most people she'd met were only interested in saying what they themselves had to say and were not interested in hearing the viewpoint of others.

She also found him physically very attractive and sexy. But, ultimately, it was the love she felt for him that was paramount – wanting to be with him every day, sharing the rest of her life with him and maybe having children together. She was getting on in terms of childbearing age so she knew there was not much time left in which she could conceive and bear a child safely and she so wanted a child. Her biological clock was ticking. She wanted a child especially from James whom she loved.

For a brief moment, submerged in these thoughts, her spirits rose slightly but then reality set in. She still found it hard to believe that the James she knew and loved was the same person who had knocked her mother down and left her in the road. How could she forgive something like that? She was not in this dilemma solely because the victim of his actions had been her own mother. She considered someone who was capable of first injuring a person with his car, then just driving off without doing anything to help, as being despicable.

It may have been true that her mother had just walked out onto the road without looking. She could be very distracted and oblivious to what was going on around her at times, because of her condition. It may also have been true that James could not possibly have avoided hitting her but what she could not understand or condone was his leaving her there and fleeing. She still found it impossible to reconcile what she knew of James with the person who had done that. He said to her that he had panicked and acted in a cowardly way because he was afraid of the consequences, but could she trust someone like that not to act in the same way in the future if he felt threatened or afraid? And what did it say about his character?

This made her think again about her own feelings of guilt. Had she not been distracted while talking to her boyfriend, her mother could well be alive today. She found it hard to forgive herself too. She should never have left her mother alone. That was done now, and could not be undone, alas!

Then it struck her. Unlikely as it seemed, her mother's death, and how it had happened, in a strange way, had created a bond between her and James – a bond of guilt. They both felt guilty about their role in it. She in one way, and he in another. She believed that he genuinely felt sorry for what he had done but, at the same time, he had never come forward to admit it, and he had told her only when she told him about her own feelings of guilt.

By this time, she was feeling emotionally drained and exhausted. She left the restaurant, making her way to the *albergue* and slept almost straight away and right through the night. When she woke the next morning, she felt somewhat refreshed. She spent some minutes lying in bed thinking about what she was going to do next. She considered calling it a day. She had set off on with such high hopes of finding a resolution to the conflict within her, and at first, it had brought her such happiness, only to have any hopes she had, dashed. She could return home. However, she also felt that having started the Camino, she should finish it, and in truth, she had even more issues to resolve now than when she started. She knew from her guidebook that there were still some one hundred and twenty-five kilometres left to reach Santiago, which would take her another five days. She was determined to finish what she had started.

She left Triacastela that morning and, later that day, reached the town of Sarria. This lay at just over one hundred kilometres from Santiago. In order to qualify for a *compostela*, one had to walk at least one hundred kilometres, so Sarria was the point from where many walkers, whose only purpose was to claim they had walked the Camino and wanted a *compostela* to prove it, started. Needless to say, it became a lot more crowded for this very reason. Maria walked on, much as she had done before, staying in *albergues* but keeping very much to herself and rarely exchanging words with anyone. The next few days were very hard. She was on her own, was still confused, and she still did not know what she wanted to do.

In Sarria, she went to Mass and prayed for a revelation of some kind, but she was still as confused and undecided as ever. The next day, after a hard walk, she reached Portomarin. It was a very welcoming little village and, despite herself and all her troubles, she was fascinated to learn that the Romanesque church in the village had been painstakingly relocated after the building of a dam on the river had flooded its original site.

Her next stop was *Palas de Rei*. As she walked, she saw and met many other pilgrims. Only once or twice did she catch sight of James. She wondered whether he was still trying to follow her. Although she did not want to talk to him, she had to admit to herself, albeit reluctantly, that she felt a certain sense of relief that he was still there, somewhere in the background. She thought about him all the time with very mixed feelings, and this made her largely oblivious to the places she was walking through, even though she sensed their beauty at times. Her nights were restless.

She woke up several times and found it hard to go back to sleep. Sometimes she would just give up, lie in bed until dawn and then rise and start walking early. The great happiness she had felt over the past weeks was completely gone. She sometimes felt that she was just going through the motions, but she still felt impelled to continue and finish what she had started. She saw the excitement and the joy of many of the younger and older pilgrims she met along the way. She could understand it completely and realised that she should have been feeling it herself having almost reached the end of the way. Yet she did not, and she felt regretful about this.

Chapter 31

James was up early. He wanted to make sure that he was ready to go when Maria came to leave the albergue. He did not want to risk losing sight of her and kept hoping against hope that she would respond to him finally. The night before, he had returned to the albergue after his dismissal by Maria and had gone straight to bed to try to drown his despair in the oblivion of sleep. Soon, he saw her go to the refectory for breakfast and he followed at a distance and sat on his own. When she had finished and headed back to the reception area to collect her rucksack, he waited till she was leaving, before picking up his own and starting off after her, at a distance.

As he walked, he thought about all that had happened in the last few hours. His whole world had fallen apart. He thought, once again, that had he kept quiet about his role in the accident, all would have been well. And yet, how could he have lived a lie with her during the rest of their lives? Every time she mentioned her mother, he would have felt a pang of guilt; every time they made love, he would have felt like an impostor and a traitor. No! It was something he had had to do. At least, he would not also be guilty of duplicity with the very person he loved.

Maria had said she needed time to think. He knew what her feelings for him were, or at least, he knew what they were before his disclosure. But now? She probably wanted to have nothing more to do with him, and the passage of time, not only would not change that, but would probably make it more likely that she would leave him for good. That was a prospect that filled him with despair. He had longed for the right woman throughout his life, one with whom he was in love, a soul partner, and Maria was that woman. Even in the short time he had known her, he was completely certain of this. How could he now accept the thought that it would all end? Not only would she leave him forever, but she would always regard him with hatred.

He wondered whether she would report him to the police in Malta. Somehow, he did not think she would do that. Perhaps her feelings for him went deep enough for her to stop short of doing that. Not that he cared anymore. Perhaps this was his punishment, after all. Losing Maria and his nemesis catching up with him. However, losing her was punishment enough. Was this how he had to atone for having caused the death of her mother? Could he not try again to make her understand and to forgive him? What a joy that would be! What a relief!

He was following her at a distance, seeing that she was walking all on her own. Hardly ever did she appear to exchange words with anyone else – a far cry from what most other pilgrims were doing. There was a very active interchange, with people ready to communicate with one another, to compare notes and to tell complete strangers their life stories. Maria kept to herself. He watched her when she stopped at roadside bars or taverns for a drink or a meal. She sat with her arms folded on the table in front of her in the way she usually did, her rucksack by her side and wearing her bandana. There was nothing he wanted to do more than to go up to her and hug her, but he could not bring himself to do it. He kept telling himself it might be too soon but the truth, deep down, was that he did not want to be rejected once more, because he felt that, with each new rejection, her refusal to ever talk to him would grow ever more entrenched. As time passed, his sense of hopelessness grew. On a few occasions, he imagined that she might have seen him following her or watching her on one of her stops, but he could not be certain, as she did not acknowledge him in any way.

In the evenings, he would follow her more closely to see where she would be stopping off for the night. He was afraid that he might lose her more easily at that time, not only because it would be dark, but because it was easier for this to happen in a town or village than in the open countryside. He would wait till she checked in to whichever *albergue* she had chosen, then, shortly after, he would check in himself. He always tried to pick a bed from where he could see her, and he would wake several times at night thinking it was morning already and he would then look to see that she was still sleeping in her bed. Thus, did he spend the nights in Sarria and Portomarin. The following day, he started off after her as usual and he stopped at *Palas De Rei* as she had done.

He was still unsure what he was going to do. When would the right moment arise so that he could talk to her, and try to break through the terrible barrier that lay between them? He was starting to get increasingly desperate. He knew that they were nearing the end of the Camino after which they would return home. He knew that would probably be the end of his chances. It occurred to him just then that there was a form of poetic justice in the pain he was suffering. It was due to the sense of loss that he was feeling – the loss of the daughter of the very person he had killed. He reached *Palas de Rei* late that evening, having followed Maria all the way. He checked into the *albergue* and went straight to bed, as he was mentally and physically exhausted.

He managed to sleep through the night but did not wake up feeling rested. He arose with some difficulty, feeling slightly out of sorts. The lack of sleep was starting to tell on him again, but he made an effort to get up, washed, dressed and made ready to leave. He saw Maria lacing her boots, then hefting her rucksack on to her back and starting off. He followed her at a distance, as usual. The Camino was very busy. There was an almost continuous stream of pilgrims following each other – a far cry from the far less busy earlier stages. While he longed for the quiet and the solitude of the less trafficked parts, there was something engaging and powerful about this stream of people, all with a common purpose moving together to the same final goal.

The Camino followed a relatively leisurely path with a gentle descent towards Melide, but it kept crossing the highway, which was a nuisance and a source of danger as it was quite busy, with heavy lorries going through. Maria stopped in one of the bars in Melide for a snack, so he did too. It was getting close to midday and he planned to stop at the next village for some lunch, if she did. When they left Melide, the path kept criss-crossing the highway. As they were entering the little village of Boente, Maria was still walking ahead of him, on her own and avoiding contact with other pilgrims.

James was following her some couple of hundred metres

further back. He had noticed that, ahead of him, was a young lady with a seven or eight-year-old boy. James had been walking some distance behind her for a while and was slowly catching up with her. He grumbled inwardly to himself as to how a mother could take a child of this age on such a demanding walk. He also noticed that the mother seemed to be very casual in the care of her little one and he worried about it, subconsciously.

They were just passing the little church in the centre of the village when James noticed with some annoyance that the mother had crossed the road and stopped to look at one of the shops. Her child carried on walking, not having realised that his mother had stopped. After a few seconds, the child turned to look for his mother and saw that she was not around. He panicked, as he could not see her anywhere. Then, he spotted her across the road some distance back and ran towards her, stepping out into the busy road. James saw him coming towards the mother who was then just across the road from him, and at the same time, he heard a fast-approaching vehicle. He realised that the mother was still engrossed in her shop window and that the child was unaware of the danger he was in. James ran towards the child to try to stop him from crossing but, by the time he reached him, he realised that there was no way they could step back on to the pavement in time.

The car was still approaching at high speed and the driver seemed to be distracted and had not noticed the child crossing the road. James ran forward and threw himself at the child, managing to push him towards the side of the road as hard as he could. A moment later, he felt himself lifted up into the air as the car hit him. The impact was shocking and, for a few moments, numbing. But then, the pain hit him with unbelievable force, and he was aware that he must be severely injured. He felt himself fall to the ground and lie still. He was unable to move even though he should have been writhing in pain, had he been able to. He was aware of people bending over him and saying things to him, which he could not understand. He tried to make out what they were trying to say but a haze had descended on him, and he was finding it impossible to concentrate. A few seconds later, he slipped into unconsciousness.

The small group of people around James saw him go limp and one of the women screamed, thinking that he was dead, while one of the men had more presence of mind and called the emergency number. The woman's scream resounded through the village street and those pilgrims who were walking ahead, turned to look back. Maria was one of them. She wondered what was going on. Who had screamed? She tried to look for the source but all she saw was a group of pilgrims who had stopped and who seemed to be trying to help someone lying on the ground.

A car had stopped in the middle of the road and the driver had come out and was gesticulating wildly. A young woman rushed towards a little boy who was picking himself off the ground and hugged him tightly. She wondered what was going on. Clearly something serious had happened – but what? She was not sure whether she should stop and go back to check. Perhaps it was some family spat and none of her business. She certainly would not want to intrude on something like that. But then, she thought of the sense of camaraderie that characterized the Camino. She should try and see what had happened and if, perhaps, she could help – if help were needed.

She walked back to the group of people and as she approached, she realised that the person lying on the ground was injured and that there was blood on the clothes. As she got closer, she saw the victim and, in that instant, she realised, to her horror, that it was James. She recognised his clothes and then saw his face. His eyes were closed, and he seemed to be unconscious. She pushed her way through the group of men who were standing around him and knelt down next to him. She lifted his head gently and put her face close to his and felt his breath. In panic, Maria screamed at the people around, "Has anyone called an ambulance?" The man who had called the emergency number replied. "Yes, *señora*, I did, and it is on the way. It should be here in a few minutes."

Maria grabbed at him and asked what had happened. He responded, emotionally, "*Señora*, he was hurt when he saved that young boy," he said, pointing at the boy who was now in the arms of his mother. "The boy ran across the road and the car was about to hit him, but the *señor* managed to push the boy out of the way in time but was hit himself."

Maria was under shock and was now trembling uncontrollably. In a few moments, she heard the sound of a siren, and an ambulance drew up with its lights flashing. A couple of paramedics jumped out and placed James on a stretcher and then carried him into the ambulance. Maria snapped out of her shock, went up to one of the paramedics and said to him, "Please, *señor*, this man is my boyfriend. I want to be with him. Please take me to the hospital with you." At first, he did not understand what she was trying to say but one of the onlookers translated. He looked at her, saw her obvious distress, and nodded to her. As they lifted James into the ambulance, she climbed in as well and sat down. The ambulance sped off immediately and she had to cling to a rail to keep herself from being thrown around, as it sped along the winding road. Her heart was pounding. They drove for just over an hour. During that time, Maria could not think of anything except that she wanted to get to the hospital as soon as possible so that James could be helped. She could see the paramedics bending over him and doing various things. One put an oxygen mask over his mouth while another was using a syringe to inject something in him. Finally, the ambulance stopped, and the doors were thrown open. James was placed on the gurney that was waiting in the emergency area and was rushed off. Maria followed quickly. There was an overpowering sense of déjà vu. The mental images of the nightmare drive to the hospital with her mother intermingled with the present.

As she ran behind the gurney, she realised that she was in a big hospital, but she did not know which one until they passed through the reception area, and she saw the sign: *Hospital Clinico Universitario de Santiago de Compostela*. As she read the sign, she thought to herself ruefully, 'We have arrived in Santiago, but certainly not in the way that it should have happened.'

The nurses pushed the gurney with increasing speed through the corridor until they got to what was clearly the operating theatre. One of the nurses told Maria that she would have to stay in the waiting area unless she wanted to go home and come back later. Maria told the nurse that she had no home, that she wanted to be there, and asked him what they were going to do to James. He replied that they would probably have to operate to treat his injuries, which seemed quite serious, but that she must not worry too much – they would do everything possible. Then they wheeled James away into the operating theatre.

Maria sat down on one of the chairs. She could not sit still and kept kneading her fingers compulsively. After some time, she looked around the room at the other occupants. They all seemed to be engrossed in their thoughts, so there was very little eye contact between them. Every so often, she would get up and pace up and down the room and the nearby corridor. Doctors and nurses kept passing by the waiting area. Occasionally, another gurney would pass by carrying another unfortunate patient into or out of the operating theatre area. She waited and waited. At intervals, she would go to the nurses' station to ask what was going on and was told each time that, as soon as there was any news, she would be informed. Finally, after what seemed like an interminable period of time, a young doctor came up to her and said,

"*Señora*, we have just finished operating on your boyfriend. He was badly injured in the accident and his condition is still unstable. He will need to stay in the intensive care unit until he is out of danger."

"Will I be able to see him, to stay with him?" asked Maria anxiously.

"Visiting is limited in intensive care but you may stay with him for one hour and a half a day, but there are strict rules you will have to follow."

"May I go to him now?" she asked.

"Soon. Once he is settled into his bed and has come round, you may see him for a very short time."

Chapter 32

They called her after some time to tell her that she could go into the ITU. She was given a surgical mask and led into the unit. She immediately sensed how quiet it was in comparison with a normal hospital ward. The nurse took her to the bed where James was lying. He was still unconscious and was connected to various monitoring devices. A pang of great sadness hit her when she saw him in this state. She prayed, 'Whatever happens between us, please Lord, let him live. I don't want him to die.'

The nurse brought her a chair and she sat and watched James anxiously. His breathing was laboured, and there was a pallor about him that really worried her. She watched the monitor plotting its regular graph of his heartbeat and other vital functions, anxiously hoping that nothing would change for the worse.

While she sat there, her mind was in turmoil. On the one hand, James was the person who had killed her mother, albeit unwittingly, and who had fled the scene of the accident and thereby, perhaps contributed further to her mother's death. On the other hand, he was the person she had dreamed about all her life. He was her soulmate, and she loved him and wanted to spend her life with him. And now, this latest twist, with his heroic action in a dire situation where a young boy could have lost his life. She felt this was more like the James she imagined that she knew. It seemed he had not hesitated in throwing himself at the boy to clear him out of harm's way, according to the Spaniard she had spoken to at the scene of the accident, and she had no reason to doubt that. That meant a lot, in her mind. It meant that in a moment of crisis, James had reacted heroically – and yet, why had he done the very opposite when faced with her mother's accident? Why on earth did he do what he did? How could the two actions be coming from the same person?

As she sat and watched his stertorous breathing, she thought to herself that within the person she admired and looked up to – and loved – there was a weakness. In a strange way, she found this almost endearing or, at least, it made her feel protective towards him. She knew that, in her case, she was guilty of carelessness. Was that any less reprehensible than fear and panic?

She was woken from her reverie by the nurse, who told her that her time was up, and she would have to leave. Maria asked her in a low voice how she thought James was getting on, and whether she thought that he would be all right? The nurse reassured her that everything was under control, and they could not do more for him than what they were doing already. Maria asked at what time she would be able to come back the next day and the nurse said that she could visit in the morning between eleven thirty and twelve, or between five and six in the afternoon.

Maria left the hospital and took a taxi to the centre of Santiago. The taxi driver dropped her off in the *Praza Obradoiro* in the heart of Santiago. When she stepped out of the taxi, the sight of the cathedral struck her. It was floodlit, dominating the square, with the relief and statuary in its façade really standing out. It was an extraordinary sight – there was something almost otherworldly about it. The square was very busy, so she walked into one of the side streets and started looking for a place to stay. After a short time, she found a small hotel in the *Plaza San Miguel*, which looked promising, and she checked in. It was still the early evening so after unpacking her things, she went out.

She walked back to the main square and from there she started to explore the rest of the city. The old, historic centre was not very big, she realised. It consisted of a dozen or so streets and several squares, but despite its small size, it was extremely vibrant. The narrow pedestrian streets were full of pilgrims celebrating their arrival in the city of St James, after their long, and sometimes harrowing, experiences on the Camino. She dined in a restaurant in the *Rua do Franco*, which was the main drag through the old centre. She sat alone, although the restaurant was full of people and really buzzing. Despite the noise, or perhaps because of it, she was able to withdraw into herself and think about her situation.

She had arrived in Santiago a couple of days before she should have, because of James's accident. She had an open ticket to return home to Malta, but it did not even occur to her to leave now. She would have to see James through his recovery first. He had no one else and, quite apart from her own, still mixed feelings towards him, she felt duty bound to stay and look after him. She would have to call up Arnold, her boss, to explain to him that she could not return as planned. She felt awkward about this because she had already taken so many weeks off. There was some comfort that, at least, Arnold did not have to do without Greta as well and she wondered how her friend was getting on. She had not spoken to Greta in the last three weeks and felt a bit guilty about that but she determined that she would call her the following morning. She would also have to call her sister, Johanna, to explain her delayed return to Malta. She had told her very little about what had been happening to her over the last weeks and, although she had mentioned James briefly in one of their telephone conversations, she had not let on how close she and James had become. She had certainly said nothing about his confession concerning their mother's death.

She wondered whether she should advise anyone in James's family about his accident. She knew that he lived alone and had no siblings, but James had mentioned a good friend he had. Maria racked her brain to try and remember his name. Was it Peter or Michael? No, she couldn't remember. Then, it suddenly came back to her – Paul – but she had no idea how she could contact him. James had also mentioned his own secretary, Lisa, and a deputy, whose name she could not remember. He had told her the name of his firm however and she made a note to look it up the next day, contact Lisa and through her, James's deputy, friend, and any family members. She had made little notes of all this on her paper napkin.

She looked up and saw that the restaurant was almost empty. While she had been deep in thought, most people had left. She suddenly felt drained. The shock she had experienced had really affected her and she wanted nothing more than to get back to her hotel, get into bed and go to sleep. As she walked through the empty, lamp-lit streets towards her hotel, she realised how very beautiful the city was.

She awoke before sunrise. She was not sure what had woken her up. The city was very quiet so she thought it must have been her anxiety about James. She was immediately wide-awake. Nevertheless, she lay in bed, trying to organise her thoughts, and planning how she would go about doing all she had to do. At seven, she rose from her bed and went down to breakfast. She knew that she could not visit James before eleven thirty, so she set about contacting the people back home to tell them about her delay in returning. Arnold was pleased to hear from her.

When she started to tell him that her return would be delayed, he was concerned at first, but when she explained the circumstances, he was quite nonplussed. He could not believe that Maria had suffered an almost identical occurrence in Spain with a boyfriend. He told her to do what she felt she had to but to try and return as soon as she possibly could, ending by saying that his thoughts were with her. She felt so grateful for his understanding and considered herself lucky to have such a considerate employer, unlike many of her friends who were constantly complaining about theirs.

Next, she phoned Johanna and told her that the man she had met on the Camino had had an accident and she felt duty bound to stay on until he had recovered. She did not tell her sister about James's disclosure as she felt that she would prefer to do that in person when she returned home. Johanna was sympathetic and certainly relieved that Maria had finally arrived in Santiago safely, and that she could stop worrying about her, although she was very curious about who this man could be, who was important enough for Maria to delay her return. When Maria got through to Greta, she already knew of Maria's delay in returning. Arnold must have told her straight away. Maria filled in the details and told her a good bit more than she had told Arnold, although, again, she stopped short of telling her of James's involvement in her mother's death.

Finally, she called James's office, having found the number on his website, and asked to be put through to Lisa. When she came on the line, Maria told her that she was calling from Santiago in Spain, that she had met James on the Camino, that he had had a bad accident and was in hospital. Lisa was shocked to hear this and bombarded Maria with questions. Maria then assured her that she would be staying on in Santiago until he had recovered sufficiently. Lisa said that James's deputy, Peter, was out of the office but she would call him straight away to tell him. Then Maria asked Lisa whether she knew the number of James's friend, Paul, so she could tell him too, but Lisa did not have it.

When Maria had finished all her calls, she decided to go for a walk around the city centre again in the daylight, as there were still a couple of hours to go before visiting time. She walked down through the *Praza Obradoiro* and climbed up the grand staircase leading to the entrance of the cathedral. When she got to the top, she turned to look at the activity in the square below. It was full of pilgrims: some, who were just arriving in the city, still laden with their rucksacks and walking poles; others, who had arrived earlier and were now celebrating their arrival. A few were lying on the floor of the square, looking up at the magnificent cathedral, while others were singing and dancing together. As she looked on, she spotted a couple of pilgrims she had seen along the way in the last few days but had not actually spoken to. Then, she saw what looked like another familiar face. For a second, she could not place it, although it looked so familiar, then it hit her – Silvia! It was Silvia. She called out, but Silvia was too far away to hear her, so Maria ran down the stairs to catch up with her before she vanished into the crowd. She just managed to reach her before she left the square and called her. Silvia turned round and Maria went up to her and hugged her tightly.

"Silvia, how wonderful to see you. I had given up hope of ever meeting you again. When we last spoke on the phone, you were some days behind us."

"Maria. Oh, Maria! It's great to see you too. I have just arrived in Santiago. After we parted, as you know, I had to slow down a bit as I was still not feeling so well, so I too had lost hope of seeing you again but then I felt better and started to walk faster and cover more distance. How have you been?"

"So much has happened since I left you. Let's go and sit at that bar, have a drink and I'll tell you all about it."

They sat on a table outside and Maria recounted to Silvia all that had happened. When Silvia heard about James's revelation of his role in her mother's death, she was shocked. Maria was wringing her hands unconsciously while she spoke, and Silvia noticed how upset she was. Finally, Maria told Silvia about the accident of the day before and that James was now in the ITU at the hospital in Santiago, and that in a short while she would be going to visit him. When she had finished her account, Silvia put her arm around Maria's shoulder.

"Maria, I am so, so sorry. I don't know what to say. It's just unbelievable – and what a shock for you."

"I'm so confused, Silvia. After James confessed to what he had done, I was horrified and wanted to leave him. Yet, at the same time, I wanted him just as badly as before. He was following me after that and never letting me out of his sight and, to be perfectly honest, I didn't want him to lose sight of me, even if I wouldn't admit it to myself, at first. After yesterday, my feelings are even more mixed up. I heard what James did from the people who saw it happen. They said that he saved the little boy by throwing himself in front of that car to push him out of its way. Not many people would have done that, and yet, he left my mother on the street after he hit her. I don't know what to do yet but the one thing I do know is that I cannot leave him here in Santiago until he is well enough to get back home."

Maria stopped and put her hands up to her face and over her eyes. Silvia was upset to see her friend so distraught and confused. She understood the very strong, conflicting forces that Maria was experiencing. She tried to imagine what she would do in a situation like that, and spent some moments thinking, before saying, with conviction,

"I agree that you should stay on here until he is better and then see how your feelings develop during this time."

Maria nodded slowly.

They went on talking. Maria asked Silvia about her own experiences but soon, it was time for her to start making her way to the hospital. Silvia asked Maria whether she wanted her to accompany her there, but Maria thanked her and declined, saying that it was something she needed to do on her own. However, they agreed to meet for dinner after the second visit of the day.

Maria walked back to the taxi rank in the main square. It was a good fifteen-minute drive to the hospital, and she did not want to arrive late, as the visiting hours were so short. She hoped and prayed that James was out of danger and starting to recover from his injuries. She had called the hospital earlier that morning, but could get no information over the phone, so she was on tenterhooks as to how he was today. She hoped that he was conscious, and that she might be able to communicate with him, although she did not expect the nurses to allow her to disturb him with any attempt at conversation.

She spoke to the duty nurse at the entrance to the ITU, was given a surgical mask to wear and then was escorted to James's bedside. He was still hooked up to various machines but, as she got closer, she saw that he was conscious. She asked the nurse how he was. She replied in halting English that he was a bit better today. He had regained consciousness early that morning and was responding well to his treatment, but it was still too early for a prognosis.

Maria approached the bed and, as she did so, she saw James turn his head fractionally to look at her. She gave him a smile of encouragement before she remembered that she was wearing a mask and he could not possibly see that, although perhaps her eyes had conveyed her feelings as a weak smile played on his face. He tried to talk but the effort was too much for him. She spoke softly to him telling him that she was not going to leave him alone and that she was going to stay on in Santiago till he was better. She saw him nod slightly and the look of gratitude in his eyes made her feel like crying. The hour was soon up, and the nurse came to tell her that her visit was over.

She spent the rest of the day wandering rather aimlessly round the city until it was time for her next visit. When she got to the hospital, James was still in much the same state although she did feel he was more responsive. Again, his look towards her caused her a great deal of emotional anguish. All too soon, the visit was over, and she made her way back to the city. She still had a few things to do before meeting Silvia for dinner.

Chapter 33

When she woke up the next morning, she thought back to her dinner with Silvia the day before. They had spent a good three hours at the restaurant and had been the last patrons to leave. Most of the time, they had talked about Maria's dilemma. Silvia had offered good, sensible advice, telling Maria not to make any rushed decisions. She fully understood Maria's antagonism towards James but at the same time, it was clear that Maria had fallen in love with him, and he with her – so how to reconcile these two intense and opposing feelings? She expressed her belief in most people's inherent sense of goodness but also in their imperfections. She put it that, while we may strive to be good, all too often we fall short of our own expectations and standards, even spectacularly so, sometimes. She said that she believed in the need for forgiveness because ultimately, all of us being imperfect, we have no choice but to forgive one another. Maria kept going over their conversation in her mind.

Silvia had told her that she was due to fly back to Rome, but that she was ready to delay her departure for a few days if Maria felt she needed any help. Maria was touched by her friend's offer and thanked Silvia, but she told her that she should return to her family, as they would all be expecting her back after a long absence. Besides, this was a journey that Maria had to undertake on her own. They had promised to keep in touch, hugged each other and then gone their separate ways back to their hotels.

On her visits to James that day, she noticed a marked improvement, both in his physical condition, as well as in the level of his response to her. As she sat near him and spoke to him softly, her mind tended to focus more on the love she felt for him rather than the antagonism and yet, after she left him, negative feelings would creep back, and she would find herself questioning whether she could ever forgive him for what he had done. After her conversation with Silvia, she had started to look squarely at the possibility of forgiveness. Was it possible and was she capable of it?

The next few days passed slowly. Every morning and every afternoon, she would visit James in the hospital. Three days after being admitted to the ITU, his condition had improved enough for the doctors to pronounce him out of danger, and he was transferred to a private room. After the first two days, he had started to converse with Maria, albeit haltingly. He still appeared to be very lethargic and found it hard to concentrate at times. The nurse explained that the medication he was taking could be causing this side effect. She kept their conversation away from anything that would upset him. There would be time to talk about more serious matters once he recovered enough.

When she was not at the hospital, she would wander round the historic centre of Santiago. She was getting to know it quite well. It was quite small, really, and it was almost all pedestrianised. The streets were narrow and many of the buildings had arcaded ground floors. She learnt that the reason for this was the fact that it rained so much in Santiago and the arcades afforded protection to pedestrians. She visited the cathedral and was struck by its simple beauty and the sense of peace it had, especially in the moments when it was not crowded with pilgrims. She knew that every day there was a Mass for pilgrims, but she had never been able to make it, as it coincided with the hospital's visiting hours. She had heard about an enormous censer called a *botafumeiro*, which was swung through the cathedral on feast days. She asked what the reason for this was and was told that it was a very old tradition that may have started to try to dispel the smell of several hundred pilgrims who, in the Middle Ages, would have been walking for weeks without washing themselves. The tradition had stuck, and today, the many pilgrims and tourists who witnessed it considered it the highlight of their visit to Santiago.

She had also discovered a couple of very good restaurants serving a wonderful selection of tapas. The fish, seafood and octopus on offer was far better than anything she had ever had. She became quite friendly with one of the waitresses who saw her there regularly. She prided herself on being able to speak English quite well – and she did – so Maria was able to ask her a lot of questions about the city and its people and traditions.

Initially, she had told herself that she could not leave James alone in Santiago until he was well enough to look after himself. He had almost reached that point. He was getting better every day and the nurses were taking him for a daily walk round the ward to avoid the risk of thrombosis. One evening, when she arrived for her usual visit, she saw a large bouquet of flowers in his room and asked him who had sent it. He told her that it had arrived that morning from the mother of the boy he had saved. She had attached a note saying that she had managed to get his name from the police and the hospital authorities following the accident and wanted to thank him with all her heart for having saved her son. She went on to say that she felt so guilty about having been distracted and having neglected to look after her son, thereby causing the accident, and that she would never forgive herself for causing James's suffering due to her negligence. She hoped that he would recover fully and quickly. She added that although she wanted to come and visit it had proved to be impossible because she had to return home the very day she arrived in Santiago.

Maria listened as James told her all this, then she asked him how it had all happened. James described the mother's distraction, the boy's sudden panic and his rushing across the road to his mother. He told her that when he saw the car approaching at speed, and with the driver clearly not aware of the boy in his path, he had acted impulsively and, without thinking, threw himself at the boy to get him out of harm's way.

James paused for a moment in his account and stopped to think, then said,

"You know, Maria, I've been thinking about this all the time. I wonder whether both actions – my saving the boy and my leaving your mother after the accident – are anomalies, in the sense that they both involved extreme situations. Perhaps the real me lies somewhere between these two extremes. I never thought I could do what I did with your mother. It is still inconceivable to me that I could have done such a thing – and yet, I did it. Thinking back, I know that I panicked at that moment and acted irrationally and very selfishly. I would understand if you could not bring yourself to forgive me, because I find it hard to forgive myself, although I do hope you will – we both will. Equally well, I find it hard to believe that I did what I did with the boy. Perhaps if I had stopped to think about it, I would have hesitated to put myself very clearly in the path of certain danger – but that too was an impulsive reaction, done on the spur of the moment and without thinking."

He paused to catch his breath, then went on,

"We humans are strange creatures, capable of performing bad or unthinking acts, but also heroic ones. We are all flawed in a sense. We all have plenty of good in us – but evil as well – and it is the balance of these, and the degree to which we are able to enhance what is good in us and to control or eliminate the evil part, that really counts. Perhaps, since we are all, or so, I believe, imperfect creatures, we should forgive each other's mistakes – mistakes, which we might perhaps find ourselves committing one day."

Maria thought to herself that James's view reflected very much what Silvia had told her the day before. She reflected on what James had said. She, too, had felt that she had fallen short and had been an unwitting cause of her mother's death. The boy's mother felt that she had caused or contributed to the accident by neglecting her son and James felt responsible for abandoning her badly injured mother on the road. In a certain sense, they were all guilty, albeit in different degrees, of a failing involving the death or injury of a person. So, could she really feel that she had the moral high ground? Could she refuse to understand and forgive someone else's failing, let alone that of the person who had unwittingly killed her mother, whom she had fallen in love with?

They spent some minutes deep in thought.

"Maria," James broke the silence finally, and with his voice breaking, said, "let me tell you once again how sorry I am for what I did. I ask you to forgive me and I pray that we can go back to where we were a few days ago. I know what we feel for each other. I know how I feel about you and, I believe, I know how you feel about me. Can we somehow live with what has happened? I know that, perhaps, it is not something you can decide now, but can you think about it? I love you and want us to make a life together. I truly believe we can, despite everything that has happened. But I place myself entirely in your hands, my love."

Maria looked at him for a long moment, "I need to think about it, James."

Chapter 34

She made her way back to the city centre to her favourite restaurant for dinner. It was quiet, and she went to sit at her usual table. Her waitress friend came to take her order and to ask her how her day had been. Maria needed to unwind a bit. She had never told anybody about her situation but today she needed to talk to someone, so she opened up to the waitress about her boyfriend being in hospital. The waitress expressed sympathy and asked Maria whether she needed any help in dealing with the hospital authorities. Maria thanked her but said it was all under control.

After she had placed her order, she started to think about all that had happened that day and about her conversation with James. What was she going to do? Before thinking about it, she wanted to call Johanna to tell her a bit more about what was going on. When she got through, Johanna asked her how things were going, and Maria said that it was a difficult time. Her boyfriend was badly injured, although he was recovering well. She did not want to tell her sister yet about James's role in their mother's death, but she did tell her that James had been walking the Camino to expiate a bad experience in his life. She told her that she would be staying on for a few more days in

Santiago until he was in a better condition. Johanna asked her how important this man was to her, since she had delayed her return home on his account. Maria replied that he might be very important, but that she needed time to think.

The conflicting feelings that she had experienced in the last few days were starting to take their toll on her. She was feeling very anxious at the uncertainty the situation had created in her life. She had listened to what James had to say and to the advice Silvia had given her. She could harden her heart and refuse to see James again, after she had performed what she considered to be her duty, in seeing him on the way to recovery. But was that the answer? She had started to see and, indeed, feel the power and righteousness of forgiveness. Then something else occurred to her. She might bring herself to forgive, but that did not necessarily mean that she would pursue the relationship with James. She felt so confused. When she finished her meal, she decided to have an early night and she started walking back to her hotel. She was exhausted, and she just wanted to get to bed and to sleep, hoping that sleeping on it would clarify things in her mind.

Life in the *Plaza San Miguel* started early the next morning, thanks to the fruit and vegetable market that had set up shop at one end of the square. Maria was woken up at six, but she felt that she had had a good long sleep and was feeling more energized than the day before. She lay in bed for a short while, thinking. However much she thought it through, she could not bring herself to hate him. She hated what he had done but loved him for what he was. The more she thought about it, the more she felt she should forgive him but then, should she maintain her relationship with him? One factor in the whole equation was her sister Johanna. She would have to tell Johanna about James and his role in the whole matter, and what Johanna thought about the whole thing was very important to her. So, she decided that she must tell her after all, and see what Johanna felt about it. She would call her sister after breakfast. She needed to prime herself for the call, so she went over all that she wanted to say, several times. Finally, she took the plunge and placed the call.

Johanna answered straight away. Maria asked her how she was and whether there had been any developments in Malta since they had spoken last. When Johanna replied in the negative, Maria told her that there was something that she needed to tell her.

"Johanna, the man I met on the Camino is Maltese as well. His name is James Borg. I didn't know him at all, and I met him quite by accident. We started to walk together and, little by little, we got to like each other – in fact, rather more than that. We spent several nights together, and I got really keen on him. I felt he was the person I had been looking for. He even proposed to me, and I accepted, because I so wanted to be with him for the rest of my life. Then, after a few days, I felt that I had to tell him about my sense of guilt because I did not want there to be anything hidden between us.

Then, I got the shock of my life. Having heard my story and realising who I was, he felt that he had to tell me that he was the very person who had run over our mother. Can you imagine how I felt? He says that he was returning home from work when mummy stepped out into the road in front of him, without any warning. At first, I just couldn't believe it but then, I felt this tremendous wrench in my guts. I loved James and yet he was the very person who ran over our mother! I couldn't bear to be with him and yet I continued to love him. I have been really torn apart these last few days. He is now in hospital because, a few days ago, he saved a young boy from being run over and, as a result, got injured himself."

She paused to catch her breath and compose herself, "This is why I have extended my stay. I could not leave him on his own in the state he was in. In the first few days, he was in intensive care, and it was touch and go whether he would make it or not. Now, thank God, he is better, has been released from the ITU and should soon be able to leave the hospital. But I still don't know what to do."

There was a long silence, then Johanna replied,

"How do you really feel about him, Maria? Is he a good person?"

"Yes. I think ... no, I am sure … that he is. He says – and I believe him – that he panicked at the moment of the accident and could not think clearly. I still cannot reconcile what I know of him with the idea of someone who could leave an injured person lying on the side of the road."

"Then why do you think he did that?"

"I think that it is as he said: that he just panicked. He says he had been driving faster than he should have been. He also says that he thought that mummy may not have been too badly injured and that she would be found quickly. He did not try, for a minute, to make up excuses or to downplay his responsibility for the accident. He feels very guilty about it and indeed, he undertook to walk this Camino to try to expiate his guilt."

Johanna stopped to think for some time, while Maria waited patiently on the line. Eventually, Johanna replied,

"Perhaps I can visualise what happened. I know that mother could be very distracted and that she could very easily have crossed the road without looking. A driver wouldn't stand a chance of being able to stop in time, especially if she crossed where we think she did, at the bend in the road. Having said that, the fact that he left the scene without trying to help is wrong and very worrying. Are you sure that you know him well enough, Maria? You only met him recently. Do you know what he is really like? Quite apart from the fact that he caused the death of our mother, I would not want you to enter into a second relationship that does not work out for you."

Maria knew that her sister loved her and did not want her to be hurt. She also knew that she could not have any feelings for James other than those generated by seeing him as their mother's killer, since she did not know him. All she knew of him was what she had just heard from Maria, who on the other hand, knew him intimately despite the relatively short time they had been together. She said very earnestly to her sister,

"Jo. I know how you must feel about all this. I know James may seem like a monster to you, but you don't know him like I do. I know that I met him only a few weeks ago, but during that time, I have come to know him well and sincerely believe that he is a good, upright person, but on that occasion, he acted out of character. In every way, he is the person I have always dreamed I wanted to be with – that is why I am so torn. At first, I was so shocked and felt so antagonistic towards him, but then I thought about it long and deeply – indeed, I have thought about little else these last days – and I really think that I want to forgive him for what he did – difficult as this may seem. What I still need to think about is whether, having forgiven him, I can also maintain the relationship with him."

Johanna thought for some moments and then said to her, "Look! I know it's been very traumatic for all of us and especially for you – and even more so now after what you have just learnt! I believe that ultimately it is something you must decide for yourself, if he means so much to you. I will go along with whatever you decide, although it will not be easy for me either."

Maria felt grateful to her sister for trying to be understanding despite what she must be feeling, and replied, "Thank you, Jo. I still need to think it through some more. Soon, hopefully, they will be releasing him from hospital, and I need to know where I am going by then. I will keep in touch. How is the family? My God! I am so wrapped up in my problems that I never even asked. How is Alex? And how are Bernard and Anthony? Do they miss their grandmother?"

"They're all well, thank Goodness. Yes, they do miss her. She was pretty close to them as her only grandchildren." As she said this, she realised that it may have been insensitive on her part as she knew that Maria missed having a family and children of her own. She kicked herself for having said it, but then continued, "They are getting on well at school and Alex recently got a promotion, so he is very pleased that his efforts have been recognised at last. I have been pretty busy at work myself and feel that I need to cut back a bit so as to spend more time at home with the boys. They are growing so fast and, before I know it, they will be grown up and ready to leave home and then, I will feel that I have missed out."

"You are really blessed in your family, Jo. I wish I had one too. It is something that I really miss, and I feel I am getting to an age when it's now or never. Anyway, give them my love and

I will be in touch soon."

After she had hung up, she first spent some time thinking about her conversation with her sister, then made her way to the hospital. James was sitting in a wicker chair in the glassed-in loggia overlooking the garden. As she approached from behind him, she saw that he was gazing out at the garden, seemingly deep in thought. She put her hand on his shoulder and he turned to face her.

"Hello, James. How are you feeling today? I must say, you are looking a lot better every day."

"Much better, Maria. I feel that I have really recovered. The doctors are quite pleased too. They told me this morning that I should be released very soon. I asked them what happens after that and they said that I will need to take it easy for a bit – no more Camino walking for the moment, I'm afraid – but after a few weeks, they think I should be back to normal."

"That's wonderful news. What will you do when you are released from hospital? Will you return to Malta straight away?"

"Maria, what I do is wholly dependent on what you decide. This morning, while sitting here, I was imagining us arriving in Santiago before any of this happened. We would have been really happy – happy to be together, happy to have finished the walk and happy to be going back to Malta to make a life together."

Maria took a chair and sat down beside him. She did not respond immediately to what James had said and they spent some minutes in silence. She thought to herself over again the thoughts that had been tormenting her, 'It has come to the crunch. James will be released very soon and I, we both, need to know what happens next. I have fallen in love with him, in a way that had never really happened before – not even with Tom at the beginning of our relationship when things were still very good between us. I know that James is the right person for me in every way – and yet, and yet ... there is the way he acted on the night he ran my mother over. I am convinced that he could not have avoided hitting her so I cannot really blame him for that, but the rest is harder to understand and to forgive. Do I accept his explanation? He did not present it as a justification for what he did. He knows he did the wrong thing but said that he panicked in that moment and ceased to think rationally. Was it an aberration due to his state of mind after the difficult time he had that day, coupled with the sudden shock of the accident? Can I bring myself to understand it? Then, on the other hand, there is his heroic action a few days ago when he risked his own life to save that boy. James had said that both actions were exceptional – and they were. After all, I too am to blame for what happened so can I really refuse to forgive him for his action?'

Finally, after a long silence, she spoke,

"James, I have been thinking about it constantly and, yes, I have come to the conclusion that I must forgive you for what you have done. What I am still struggling with is whether I can bring myself to resume our relationship, much as I would like to do so. Indeed, there is nothing I would like to do more."

"Then why not do what your heart tells you?" James said with a broken voice. "I understand your feelings about what I did, and I cannot pretend that I am not responsible for what I did, but believe me when I say, once again, how truly sorry I am. But I really believe that we have found each other, and I think it would be tragic if we were to lose each other now."

Maria looked at him. She saw the pleading and desperation in his eyes. She sensed the slumping of his shoulders as he spoke. She thought again to herself, 'If I am ready to forgive him – and I do believe that is the right thing to do – then why not do what my heart and mind tell me that I want and need? My life would fall apart if I were to leave him now and I don't think I would ever forgive myself. She felt a sudden and irresistible surge of feeling for him. She took his hands in hers and felt their warmth, pulled him towards her, put her arms around him and pressed him tightly against her. She held him like that for a very long moment, then she released him, saying,

"James, I cannot live without you either, despite everything that has happened. I love you and I want to be with you. I believe that what happened on that terrible night was something extraordinary and exceptional and I want to try and put it behind us for ever."

He looked at her in joyful disbelief and then said, with great feeling, "Oh! Maria. What unbelievable joy this gives me! I too, want to spend the rest of my life with you, loving you."

They sat there for a long time, just holding each other until visiting hours were over.

Chapter 35

After Maria left, James felt he was walking on air. He was feeling enormous relief at the thought that, not only was Maria ready to forgive him, but she still felt as strongly about him as he did about her. The gloom and depression he had been in over the last days suddenly evaporated as though they had never been. He felt renewed physically as well and looked forward impatiently to his release from the hospital.

Sure enough, when the doctors came to visit him on their rounds the next morning, they thought he was fit to leave, and told his nurse to prepare him to be discharged. Soon after, she went through his medication regime with him and provided him with a first batch of the pills he would be taking. She also went over the physiotherapy exercises that he was to self-administer and gave him a contact number in case he needed any help.

When Maria arrived for her usual morning visit, he told her that he was about to be released that same day. She was pleased to hear this and asked him whether his movement would be restricted at first, but he told her that, other than taking it easy, getting plenty of sleep and following his treatment regime, he could move around. They immediately set about making plans for what they would do over the next few days. Maria suggested, and James agreed, that they spend at least a couple of days in Santiago. Having walked very nearly all the way there, and having experienced its allure, Maria really felt that they should spend a short while there before returning to Malta. She told James that she was staying in the hotel in the *Plaza San Miguel* and she would ask to exchange her single room for a double.

While he was being readied to leave, she went for a little stroll in the garden adjoining the hospital. It was a small oasis of peace in an otherwise busy part of the city. As she walked, she thought to herself how very relieved she felt. Despite all her misgivings about what James had done, deep down, she had never really wanted to leave him. She was far too deeply in love with him. She felt that, with time, she would be able to reconcile her love for him with the antagonism she had been feeling since he had first told her about his role in the accident. From where she stood, there was a panoramic view of the city with the twin spires of the cathedral dominating it and she experienced once again the feelings that the city had produced in her, feelings that she wanted to share with James.

When she went back to James, he was all set to leave so they thanked his nurses and made their way to the exit to get a taxi back to the city centre. They had no problem exchanging Maria's single room for a double, and after Maria had repacked all her things, they were shown to their new room. When they were alone at last, James went up to Maria, put his arms around her and moved his face towards hers. She responded and they kissed long and passionately but when Maria sensed that James wanted to go further, she put her fingers gently over his mouth and said to him, "Not now, James. I want this too, but let's wait till tonight." With great reluctance, James let her go. After he had unpacked his things, Maria suggested they go for a slow stroll in the main square.

The *Praza de Obradoiro* is the heart of the old city. On three sides of it, there are palatial buildings like the *Hostal de los Reyes Catolicos* – a mediaeval hostel for princes and nobles, now turned into a five-star hotel under the Parador banner, and the *Palacio* Rajoy. However, the most spectacular was the cathedral on the east side of the square with its very ornate façade, which dominated the square and indeed, the whole city. James gasped when he saw it. It had this effect on many people seeing it for the first time.

He wanted to go in and visit it, but Maria said that they should enter by the side entrance on the east side since this would avoid his having to climb the long flight of steps on the piazza leading up to the main entrance. They were both struck by the activity in the square. There were large groups of pilgrims who had just arrived in the city and had stopped in the square, spellbound, groups of tourists who were being taken on walking tours, and the townspeople who were going about their business in an ordinary way.

James remarked to Maria that he could hear bagpipes playing in the distance and she told him that, on most days, there was a solitary bagpipe player standing under the arch to the side of the square, playing through most of the day. She told him that she had read that Galicia was one of the original Celtic settlements in the western part of Europe and its people shared the love of bagpipe music with other countries with a Celtic background, like Scotland. The music he played was quite plaintive, but it created a very powerful atmosphere, in and around the square. They walked on to the *Praza de Quintana* on one side of the cathedral from where they could enter without going up a large number of steps.

The interior of the cathedral had the same effect on James as had the exterior. At that hour, there were very few people inside, so they could really experience the sense of peace and serenity. Maria took him round and showed him the famous *Portico de la Gloria* at the main entrance – a marvellous Romanesque sculptured portal that had just been restored. Then she took him round the various chapels in the aisles and in the apse, and finally to the effigy of Saint James behind the great altar, which pilgrims were queuing to go up to and embrace.

They sat down in one of the pews to take it all in and James suddenly felt a great rush of gratitude to think that, after all that had passed, he was being given a second chance. On an impulse, he knelt and started to say a prayer of thanksgiving. Maria watched him. She sensed what he was feeling and, because this mirrored what she herself was experiencing, she too knelt beside him and prayed. The cathedral started to fill up and soon it was full to bursting with people and they realised that a Mass was about to start. They looked at each other and then nodded in tacit agreement as they decided to stay on for it.

They were both very moved by the Mass. The whole congregation participated wholeheartedly in the celebration, despite the great variety of nationalities, faiths and ages. A small, solitary nun, with a voice that belied her diminutive size, led the singing, accompanied by the great organ. As the Mass neared its end, they both sensed an air of expectation among the congregation, as a group of six or seven men, dressed in burgundy-coloured uniforms, stepped up to the altar and lowered the very large censer that was hanging from the dome. Each one held a separate cord connected to the rope which, in turn, ran up to the pulley just below the dome from which the censer was hanging. Maria whispered to James that this was the famous *botafumeiro,* which was swung through the transept of the cathedral, giving him the whole background on its origin. One of the men started it swinging and then, in unison, they all tugged on their cords and, as they did so, the censer suddenly rose several metres and started to swing more widely.

This went on for several minutes with the men tugging and then releasing the cords until the censer was swinging through the transept, practically touching the roof at either end of its swing, while discharging clouds of incense. Meanwhile, the great organ was playing at full volume while the choir sang a very rousing hymn. It was a spectacular sight and they, and everyone else in the cathedral, stood watching, enthralled. Then the oscillations reduced, the censer slowly descended to the ground, the organ stopped playing and the service was over. They spent a few more minutes just assimilating the whole experience and then, hand in hand, they walked out of the cathedral, feeling quite moved by it all.

It was getting late, and they were both hungry, so they decided to have an early dinner. Maria took him to her favourite place and introduced him to her waitress friend, who complimented him on finally being out of hospital. Between her and Maria, they chose a selection of Maria's favourite tapas. The restaurant was full, but they were sitting in one corner that was quieter and somewhat segregated from the rest of the area by some large plants, so they felt that they had their own little, private space. While they waited for their order to arrive, they talked about the other-worldly experience they had had in the cathedral, then James took Maria's hands in his and told her how he felt reborn after feeling that all had been lost, and how he was now looking forward to the future. She, in turn, told him that she too felt so relieved that they were together again, but she also told him what a struggle it had been for her to reconcile the accident with what she knew of and loved about him. She told him about her conversation with her sister, Johanna who, once again, had shown how understanding she could be. This led to James asking about her sister and her family and she started to tell him her whole life story or, at least, those parts of it that she had not already told him. He said that he looked forward to meeting her sister as her only close relation, one who clearly loved Maria and did her very best to look after her younger sister.

They finished their meal, agreeing about how great it had been. They were both feeling a warm glow from the food they had eaten and the wine they had drunk. As they downed their cups of coffee, James told her,

"Maria, let's go back to the hotel now. I want to kiss you and make love to you so badly! I cannot wait any longer."

Their lovemaking was ecstatic. After the terrible days when both of them had been convinced that it was all over, now, after their reconciliation, they both felt a poignant mixture of relief and longing. They held each other tightly while they made love as though they both feared to lose each other again. When it was over, they just lay in each other's arms for a long time, feeling the warmth of their bodies. James stroked her face and ran his fingers through her hair, and they whispered little endearments to each other until finally, they both fell asleep.

Chapter 36

The noises coming from the square woke them both early, next morning. James woke up a bit before Maria. They were both still lying in the same position in which they had dropped off to sleep the night before, their bodies intertwined and their faces a few inches away from each other. James looked at her and thought to himself how grateful he was that Maria was ready to forgive him, even if he still found it hard to forgive himself. He realised what a rare quality that was, for someone to forgive the author of her mother's death. Whoever it was had to be very special. Many people he knew would not even forgive offences much less grievous than that. Much as he was so pleased that this had happened, he still wondered whether he deserved it. He recalled that he had set off on this Camino with a view to somehow atoning for his actions. Had he really achieved this? Yes, there had been some considerable physical effort and discomfort at times, but he had only experienced real pain when he thought that he had lost Maria forever. But perhaps the processes of atonement and forgiveness were intertwined and inseparable.

While still deep in thought, he sensed that Maria was starting to awaken. Her eyelids flickered briefly and then she opened her eyes languidly and spent some moments looking at James before fully realising where she was. Then she shook herself awake and kissed him softly.

"Good morning, my love. How wonderful it was last night. I felt like I was being reborn, coming back to life after despair!" James greeted her, with feeling.

"Yes, I too felt the same way. From the moment I saw you after the accident and then, in the ITU, I was terrified that I could lose you too," she replied.

They lay there for some more time, speaking little and just experiencing their closeness. Maria was thinking about the way things had turned out. She was also thinking hard about something else that was very much on her mind, but she did not mention it to James. Instead, after a time, she roused him and told him that they should get up and go and have breakfast. She was famished after all the exercise the night before and wanted to show James more of this city, which she had grown to love.

After their breakfast in the hotel, they walked down to the cathedral square and then she took him on a little tour of the old city. They visited the cathedral museum where a copy of the famous *Liber Sancti Jacobi*, which formed part of the *Codex Calixtinus,* was kept. It was said to be the earliest guide of the Camino and dated back to the twelfth century. It was a beautiful, illuminated manuscript that recorded the experiences of Aymeric Picaud, the French monk who had written it. He had walked the Way and written a detailed account of it. Then she took him through many of the narrow, arcaded streets and little squares and finally they visited the great monastery of *San Martin Pinario*. They stopped for lunch and while waiting for their meal to arrive, she told him that they should really visit

Finisterre – or Fisterra, as it was known here in Galicia. This was regarded, in antiquity, as being the very end of the earth, since it was one of the westernmost points of continental Europe bordering the Atlantic Ocean. In the past, when pilgrims reached Santiago, it was not the end of the road for them. They were expected to walk on to Finisterre, a further ninety kilometres or so. Once they got there, they would discard their clothes in the Atlantic Ocean before donning new ones, to symbolise a new beginning. James warmed to the idea as she described it. Of course, they would have to take a bus to get there, as walking any great distance was out of the question for James, at least for the moment.

When they finished their meal, they walked to the nearby bus station, asked about buses to Finisterre and found out that one was due to leave in fifteen minutes. They boarded the bus and it left shortly after. At first, the route passed through rolling hills, very similar to the countryside they had walked in last, but then it reached the coast, and it followed the rugged coastline till they got to the town of Finisterre, where the bus stopped them. They asked how they could get to the actual peninsula and were directed to a taxi rank close by. The taxi driver they spoke to said that it was a fifteen-minute drive to the peninsula and after they agreed the price, they got in.

The road rose up the side of the precipitous headland that jutted out beyond the town into the wild Atlantic. When they got to the top, the taxi stopped, and the driver indicated that he could go no further and told them they would have to walk the short, final stretch. They could see a lighthouse close by and he told them that they would need to walk just beyond that for the best view of the setting sun.

As they passed the lighthouse, the whole panorama was suddenly visible. They were standing on the top of the peninsula, which sloped steeply downwards before plunging vertically into the sea far below, where the waves were crashing against the cliffs. There was a large number of people sitting on the rocky slopes. Some had brought little snacks or sandwiches, some were reading their books, but they were all waiting for the sunset. One or two of the people were strumming on a guitar and singing softly, while someone was playing on a mouth organ.

Maria and James found a comfortable spot on some smooth rocks facing westwards and they sat down. The view was spectacular! The shimmering sea stretched out to the horizon on three sides of the peninsula while, on the landward side, the rugged Galician coastline vanished into the distance. Sea gulls and other marine birds were flying up from the sea and soaring above the steep slopes, filling the air with their wild cries. There was a strong breeze blowing in from the west and there were wisps of cloud in the sky. James thought to himself that there was no other land between where they were sitting, and the coast of America, thousands of kilometres away.

Maria was thinking about what she had read in her guidebook about ancient druidic rites taking place in this magical spot. Slowly the sun sank lower and lower, and the sky first turned golden, then red, with the clouds reflecting the red light. There was an air of expectancy among the onlookers, and a few stood up to get a better view or, perhaps, in awe at the spectacle. As the sun dropped to the horizon, it appeared to flatten and dilate and then, as it started to dip below the horizon, the sky went through the whole spectrum from red and orange, through green, blue and indigo to deep purple, turning ever darker. Everyone was spellbound by the sight.

Maria and James sat there holding hands long after the sun had set. James thought back to what Maria had told him about the significance of the end of the Camino, about pilgrims leaving behind their old selves and donning new clothes and being purified. People were starting to leave, and they too got up reluctantly to start making their way back. They returned to the point where they had been dropped off and found a taxi to take them back to Finisterre. On the way back, Maria asked James whether he felt up to the bus ride back to Santiago and he replied that he was feeling on top of the world in more ways than one, so they boarded the bus. It was fairly late when they got back to the city, but they were both hungry, so they made for Maria's favourite restaurant. It was almost full, but they found a quiet corner table all to themselves, away from the general hubbub, and huddled up together.

James took Maria's hand in his and said to her, "You know you told me that pilgrims would discard their clothes once they got to Finisterre and change into new ones to symbolise a new beginning in their lives. Well, we went there together today, and I feel that in that vast ocean, I left behind my old clothes – all the used and dirty old clothes that I had – and now I want to make a new beginning with you. Will you take me, Maria?"

Maria looked at him for a long moment with an unusual expression on her face, then said, "Yes, James. I will take you. That is what I want too."

She paused for a moment or two and then continued, "It is a new beginning in more ways than one." She looked James squarely in the eyes, and went on, "There is something else that you should know. Some ten days ago, my period was due, but it never came. While I was in Santiago and you were in hospital, I went to see a doctor and she carried out some tests. Yesterday she called me to tell me the result," she paused for effect, with a wide smile on her face.

"And…?" James asked, with bated breath.

"Yes, I am pregnant. It must have been that wonderful first night we spent together in Leon. We are going to have a baby."

"Hooray!" James couldn't contain himself. He shouted it out and almost jumped to his feet and the people on the other tables turned around to look at them. "That is the most wonderful news imaginable, Maria. I can't believe it. It's fantastic!" He was practically dancing on his feet while still semi-seated at the table.

"Don't tell everyone in the restaurant about it," Maria said smiling. "Yes, it is wonderful news, and I am over the moon, and let me make it absolutely clear that it had nothing to do with my decision to forgive you and to continue our relationship. I would have done it anyway."

James gave her a big hug and then said, more calmly, "Well, we must really celebrate this wonderful news." He beckoned to the waitress and, when she came, he asked for a bottle of their best champagne. The waitress looked at them both and smiled. When the champagne arrived, accompanying it was a small dish with the famous local almond cake known as the *Tarta de Santiago*, with the cross of St James moulded into the top surface.

"This is with our compliments," said the waitress. "Something to go with your champagne."

They thanked her profusely for the thought and after she

popped the cork, she poured them a glass each and wished them well for whatever it was they were celebrating.

As they clicked their glasses together, Maria said, "Let's drink to us, to our new beginning and to the new life that is growing inside me."

They were almost the very last to leave the restaurant. Even the Spaniards had left, which was saying something. They were both very excited and talked about myriad things but mainly about their return to Malta, to a life together and about the birth and future of their unborn child. They headed back to their hotel through the nearly empty streets but, when they got to the *Praza de Obradoiro*, they heard music and singing. On one side of the square, under the arcades of the Palacio Rajoy, there was a large group of people watching a group of musicians playing. They went closer and saw that the musicians were dressed up in traditional costumes. They were strumming their guitars and mandolins and singing.

Both James and Maria realised, at the same moment, that it was another group of the same *La Tuna* they had both seen separately in Logroño the evening before they met. They stopped to watch and very soon they got carried away by the music. They recognised a few of the songs being sung, although many were completely new to them, but all were played with such verve and excitement that everyone was clapping or swaying in time to the music. Despite the lateness of the hour and their tiredness, they stayed on till the very end.

As they left, James put his arm round Maria and said to her, "How strange, and wonderful at the same time, that we should have happened on that again. The first time was just before we met, when we experienced it separately and now again, at the end of our Camino, when we experienced it together."

"Yes, I was also thinking the same thing," Maria agreed, as she rested her head on his shoulder. She paused for a minute before going on, "This Camino has been a life-changing experience. Meeting you and falling in love and then that terrible interlude when I didn't want to see you and then, your accident. Then, thank Goodness, our getting back together again, and, most important of all, our child." She paused again, a little breathless, " …and, of course, the walk itself, has been so unforgettable. It's a pity that we did not actually manage to finish it, having got so very close to the end."

"You know, Maria, one day we should return and finish it off and collect our *Compostela* – not that that is so important – but it would be nice to have one after all the effort."

"Yes, we will do that," Maria replied, her eyes shining "and we will start again from Leon, where we spent our first night together and where I believe our baby was conceived and walk the way again from there to Santiago and the last stretch will be very different to what it was this time."

Maria and James slept late the next morning after the very long and eventful day they had had. Their flight back to Madrid was due to leave at midday and from there, they would then catch their flight back to Malta. They packed their rucksacks for the last time and waited till the taxi they had ordered came to pick them up. As they drove through the city on their way to the airport, they saw new groups of pilgrims streaming past, most of them with expressions of excitement and anticipation as they walked their last few steps towards their objective. At the airport, there were also many more pilgrims on their way back home. Most of them wore expressions of contentment as they discussed experiences among themselves.

While they waited for their flight to be called, James thought back to the long road that had brought him here. What a journey it had been! Starting with despair and a great sense of guilt, then walking on his own and then that most fortuitous meeting with Maria. He remembered how they had walked together for days, gradually falling in love without ever realising what lay between them and then, the terrible moment of disclosure when their world came crashing down. Then, Maria's caring for him after the accident and, blessedly, her forgiveness and the unbelievably wonderful news of Maria's pregnancy. He wondered to what extent his saving the boy had played a part in her forgiving him. He had set off on the Camino hoping to atone for his actions and to find forgiveness. He had, indeed, found forgiveness and from the very person from whom it meant the most. Of course, there was Maria's sister from whom he would hope to receive forgiveness as well.

'Would she forgive him?' he wondered. That was something he would have to face when he got back to Malta. He wondered, too, whether he could forgive himself without paying the price for his actions, and he asked himself whether he should ultimately own up to the crime once he got back. That might help to assuage the guilt he still felt within himself, despite Maria's unconditional forgiveness.

Maria noticed that James was deep in thought. She too had been reminiscing about the events that brought them together. Last night's second encounter with *La Tuna* made her feel there was something preordained in the way things had turned out. She too, thought about the events of the last months, starting from the tragic death of her mother and her great sense of guilt, the decision to walk the Camino to find resolution, her meeting with James and all that followed and now, unbelievably, her pregnancy. She felt such a great sense of fulfilment and excitement when she thought of that. She looked again at James, who still seemed to be somewhat perturbed by whatever was on his mind, and she asked him what was troubling him.

With a deep sigh, he replied, "I have been thinking about all that has happened in these last few months since the accident. I feel so utterly grateful for your forgiveness and so relieved that we are back together, but I still find it hard to forgive myself and I was wondering whether I should own up to the police, and confess my role in the accident, when we return to Malta. I don't know what it will mean, but I sometimes wonder whether I need to do this in order to fully resolve my sense of guilt. I have also worried about whether your sister will forgive me too."

"Listen, dear. I know Johanna and what an understanding and generous person she is, so I am sure that she will forgive you. I have told her about you, about all that has happened, and I do believe that she will forgive you and that, in time, she will grow to love and respect you too. As for admitting to the police, what will that achieve? Johanna and I are the injured parties and if we forgive you, why put yourself in that position?" Maria replied, suddenly anxious.

"Well, it's perhaps my sense of justice and the need for retribution for my wrongdoing," he replied.

"We are going to have a baby in less than nine months from now. I would not want to be without my husband at this most special time. There is, perhaps, another way in which you can find peace. Our child will be the grandchild of my mother. She would have been ecstatic about her next grandchild. You will be instrumental in bringing him or her up to be a decent and responsible person."

Then she said, with great conviction, "That is the Way!"

Printed in Poland
by Amazon Fulfillment
Poland Sp. z o.o., Wrocław

28953167R00157